Beta Dixon Holsteen is more than ready to leave behind Savannah, Georgia and the problems facing the Shifter Council. He misses the beauty of his mountain home and the bonds he's forming in his pack. After returning to the council's headquarters for one last meeting, Dixon stops at the cafeteria to get a bite to eat before heading to the airport. To his surprise, he scents his mate in a big polar bear shifter bussing tables. He learns Helsinki Akna had been picked up while in the company of a rogue ex-councilman. Speaking with the big, shy man, Dixon realizes quickly that it wouldn't take much for someone to manipulate the soft-spoken bear. His mate is a bit . . . dim. Still, Dixon knows that finding a fated mate is a gift, and he wants him. When Dixon makes his intentions known, Helsinki is confused, being under the belief that Fate doesn't create same-sex matings. Some of those who Helsinki associates with reinforce that opinion. Can Dixon convince Helsinki they truly are meant for each other while extricating him from the unhealthy influences he's been under for years?

Luring the Polar Bear
Copyright © 2020 Charlie Richards
ISBN: 978-1-4874-3096-2
Cover art by Angela Waters

Published by eXtasy Books Inc or
Devine Destinies, an imprint of eXtasy Books Inc

Look for us online at:
www.eXtasybooks.com or www.devinedestinies.com

Luring the Polar Bear
Wolves of Stone Ridge: Book Fifty-Three

By

Charlie Richards

DEDICATION

To those who accept that we all make mistakes. To err is human, no matter how much we strive for perfection. Thank you for joining me on my journey anyway.

CHAPTER ONE

R ubbing the bridge of his nose, Beta Dixon Holsteen did his best to pay attention. He would rather have been anywhere but at the ex-councilmen's trials. For expediency, both ex-councilman Paraben Krakow and ex-councilman Sasha Delaney were being tried at the same time. Along with them were some of their top leaders—well, the ones who hadn't died in the fighting, anyway.

"This is a farce!"

Dixon couldn't help it. Upon hearing Paraben's outburst, he rolled his eyes. The wolf shifter would never accept any opinion but his own.

"I am a councilman," Paraben claimed, standing tall behind the podium despite the chains around his wrists and ankles. "My actions are above reproach, and you are the ones deserving punishment for attempting to stop me from strengthening our people."

"For the love of the gods," Councilman Nigel Granis grumbled. "Shut the fuck up, Krakow. No one gave you permission to speak."

Paraben pinned a hate-filled stare on the Siberian tiger shifter.

Nigel ignored him in favor of glancing at the other six councilmen—each of a different shifter species, some predator and some prey. "Are we ready to call a vote?"

"We are," Councilman Regales Colearian, a grizzly shifter, stated gruffly, his honey-brown eyes holding a steely gleam.

"Thumbs down for death. Thumbs up for leniency." Then Regales lifted his own hand and pointed down.

In swift, steady succession, each councilman lifted a hand and made a thumbs down motion. The final councilman, Georgio Peregrine—an elk shifter who had supported Paraben's views in the past—slowly lifted his hand. His expression turned pained.

"I am sorry, Paraben," Georgio murmured, his voice holding a wealth of sorrow. "I believed in your views for years, but"—he pointed his thumb toward the floor—"I have learned over the last couple of years that our views are antiquated." Then his features hardened. "And I could never support someone selling our kind to humans to be tortured, gay or not."

While Sasha's already fair features paled even more, leaving him a pasty shade, and a shudder racked through the coyote shifter, Paraben snarled and lunged toward Georgio. The chains stalled him for only a brief second, snapping with a resounding crack. Paraben began to shift, murder gleaming in his green eyes.

Dixon jumped from his seat.

Before Dixon could even begin to shift, a heavily muscled blond who'd been standing at the wall moved even faster. He jumped at the shifting Paraben. In mid-air, he changed into a massive komodo dragon.

The dragon landed on top of the still-morphing Paraben. In a swift move, he wrapped his jaws around the almost-wolf and jerked his head. With a resounding snap and a sickening squelch, the komodo snapped Paraben's neck while tearing out his throat.

Georgio trembled even as he sat back down, having risen at some point, probably intending to flee, considering the panicked scent rolling off the elk shifter.

"Thank you, Enforcer Delanrue," Councilman Lorian

Bakerman, a buffalo shifter, stated gruffly. His dark brown eyes narrowed as he pinned his gaze on a clearly sweating Sasha. "Are you going to fight, Sasha? Or accept your fate with dignity?"

Sasha's nostrils flared as he straightened. His eyes narrowed even as the acrid scent of his fear filled the large room. After swallowing hard enough to cause his Adam's apple to bob, Sasha took a step forward.

"Your changing values are like quicksand that will suck the shifter race under, making us vulnerable to the *humans*," Sasha stated coldly, spitting the last word out like a curse and pinning his spiteful gaze on Theo, the human mate of Councilman Regales Colearian. "Paraben may have discovered a way to hide his lies, but the humans have the same ability." Scoffing, Sasha sneered. "Somehow, that human has tricked you into thinking he's your fated mate. Best discover the means of this ability, or it will be the downfall of our race." Then Sasha spat on the floor in Theo's direction. "May Fate make you rue the day you discarded our guidance."

Regales curled his lip in a snarl, his big hands tightening on the arms of his chair.

Dixon guessed only Theo's hand on Regales's shoulder kept the councilman from rising.

In a droll voice, Councilman Aiden Ridgeston commented in his British accent, "We'll be sure to take that under advisement." Then the deer shifter focused on the komodo dragon enforcer. "If you would carry out the sentence, Enforcer Delanrue."

Without a second of hesitation, Enforcer Delanrue advanced on Sasha. The other shifter's eyes widened with fear, and he took a step backward. The enforcer didn't give the ex-councilman time to take another.

Enforcer Delanrue pounced on Sasha, taking him to the black marble floor of the sentencing room. The dragon sank his teeth into the other shifter's throat and tore it out with ease, swiftly ending Sasha's life. After Delanrue spat the flesh out, he moved toward the wall where his stoic-faced brothers waited.

While Dixon hadn't been introduced to everyone in the trio, he'd heard the stories. The three Drudeson brothers were all komodo dragon shifters, all enforcers, and were damn loyal to the council. Each differed in small ways.

Enforcer Delanrue was the oldest and the most serious. He worked as a council interrogator, and he had no qualms about using questionable and brutal methods to get the answers he wanted from someone. Everyone who spoke of him scented just a little of fear when they talked about his abilities.

The middle brother—Enforcer Dane—was good friends with Councilman Regales. He worked as a personal guard to the grizzly shifter whenever he was in the council building. His disposition came across as intense but not as intimidating. Dixon had spoken to him a few times and found his confidence attractive.

The youngest brother—Enforcer Dakota—had accompanied Councilman Regales when he'd visited the Stone Ridge wolf pack. Dixon hadn't been there at the time, but those who'd met him told Dixon that Dakota was friendly and approachable. Watching Dakota interact with others, Dixon decided they were right . . . unless he was guarding a councilman. Then he was just as serious as his brothers.

"This concludes our business today," Councilman Lorian stated before rising to his feet. "At last." Then the big buffalo shifter lifted his arms over his head, stretching his back.

The others started doing the same, so Dixon did as well. He spotted Enforcer Dakota and Enforcer Germaine—some kind of snake shifter, judging by his scent—head to the bodies. Enforcer Delanrue returned to human form, uncaring of his nudity, which was typical of shifters.

4

"Ready to go, Beta Dixon?"

Dixon turned and focused on Manon Lemelle. The wolf shifter was one of the Stone Ridge pack's enforcers. Manon had joined Dixon as well as a number of others when head enforcer Carson Angeni had arrived at Alpha Declan's home with news of the rogues' intention of attacking a councilman's estate.

It had been an honor—and a little fun—to help stop the bastards and round up the traitors to their kind.

Opening his mouth, Dixon prepared to agree to leaving. Then his stomach growled. "Actually, I think I'd like to stop at the cafeteria," he stated instead. "I could use something to eat before heading to the airport."

Manon smirked at him, his slate gray, nearly black eyes twinkling. "Watching rogues' throats be torn out work up an appetite for you, Beta?" he teased with an almost feral-looking grin.

Heading toward the door, Dixon shrugged. "What can I say? I'm a little blood-thirsty when it comes to protecting our kind."

"Me, too," Manon replied gruffly. His mirth faded as he grumbled, "Those bastards would have happily sold those like me and my mate to scientists." Peering back at the dead ex-councilmen, Manon snarled, "No way I not be happy dat dey get what dey deserve. No one gets near my Chris."

Dixon smiled grimly as he followed Manon's focus, noticing how one enforcer unwound a hose attached the wall while others carried the dead ex-councilmen from the room. *Huh. Now the drains make sense.* The thickening of Manon's Cajun accent told Dixon just how vehemently the enforcer felt about his words. It wasn't surprising, really, since if Dixon had a mate, he would feel just as protective.

Resting his hand on Manon's shoulder, Dixon guided him toward a door. "I hear you, my friend." As they exited the room, he searched for a new subject. "Is Chris waiting at the airport for you? I suppose we could snag something on the road, instead, if you're in a hurry."

Manon would probably be in a hurry to get back to his mate, Christopher Peterson.

"Naw, we can hit the cafeteria," Manon replied, turning left to head in that direction. "Chris and a few other guys are checkin' out some of the popular sites in Savannah, since we didn't know what time the trial would wrap up." Pulling his phone out, he waved it while grinning. "We'll tell them a time to meet at the airport. Having access to a private jet has its perks, eh? We can make our own flight schedule."

"That is definitely nice," Dixon acknowledged, releasing Manon's shoulder. "How did Alpha Declan get in so good with the Vampire Council that they would loan him one of their jets?"

"Vince Marché called in a few favors," Manon told him. "That way, the rogues thought it was vampires flying out here, not shifters intending to help."

Dixon nodded absently, wondering how he'd missed that in the briefing. Vince was an enforcer for the Vampire Council, mated to the wolf, Frankie Drunger, a member of Declan's pack. It made sense for the vampire to pull some strings, since stopping the rogues helped all paranormals.

After almost three years as the Stone Ridge pack's beta, Dixon was still learning the relationships of everyone. There were a lot of members to meet. Some nights, his mind reeled after sitting through meetings at Alpha Declan's side.

Entering the cafeteria, Dixon peered around the large space. He spotted many half-full tables and realized he hadn't been the only one at the trial interested in food. Seeing Alpha Kontra Belikov sitting with Councilman Vincentius Goldstein—the councilman whose home had been attacked— Dixon headed that way.

Alpha Kontra was a bear shifter who led a semi-nomadic biker gang. A number of his people had joined in not only defending Vincentius's home but also in a sneak attack on the warehouses the rogues were using as a base. The alpha's beta, Sam Abbott, sat with them.

"Let's see what's on the buffet before we sit," Dixon stated as he passed the table. He smiled at the group, nodding to several of them in deference to their higher station. "You mind if we sit with you in a minute?"

Vincentius waved at the empty seats. "Feel free. I'd like the opportunity to thank you and your people again."

"No thanks needed," Dixon countered, grinning. "It was our pleasure." Then he waved and headed toward the buffet. "Be right back."

Manon followed.

As Dixon crossed the room, a scent other than the food teased his nostrils. The pleasing aroma caused his blood to heat, and an unexpected bloom of arousal made his gut clench. He inhaled, but by the next step, the smell was gone.

Shaking his head, Dixon frowned and continued on. He stopped at the end of the buffet and picked up a tray. After placing a plate and roll of silverware on it, Dixon started toward the food.

Except, that same smell distracted him — strong, thick, and clearly masculine.

Dixon's mouth watered for a whole new reason. His dick plumped behind the fly of his jeans. His heart rate sped up.

Freezing, Dixon tipped his head back and took a deep breath. He barely managed to swallow his moan. The delicious aroma was close.

"You all right?" Manon asked softly, a look of concern on his face.

Am I? What's going on with me?

Then the realization hit him like a two-by-four upside the head.

Meeting Manon's gaze, Dixon muttered in shock, "I think I scent my mate."

Manon's dark eyes widened but only for an instant. Then a wide smile curved his lips. He glanced around as if he would be able to tell who it was.

"That's great, Beta Dixon," Manon stated, returning his focus to him. "I think everyone in here is a shifter. Should make claiming him or her easy, right?"

Dixon snorted, shaking his head. "You really think so? Finding my mate *here*?" He set his tray down, no longer interested in food. "The prevalent opinion until recently was that Fate didn't make homosexual pairings, and the scent is definitely masculine. Thank the gods."

"Want me to whip you up a tray while you track down the source?" Manon offered. "Maybe you can have a meal with the guy and get to know him."

"Thanks, Manon," Dixon murmured distractedly, surveying the area. "I appreciate it."

Manon patted him on the shoulder. "Good luck."

Nodding absently, Dixon moved away from the buffet. He wandered slowly around the room, changing direction when the fantastic smell grew fainter. Tracking the scent in the large, air-conditioned cafeteria ended up being more difficult than Dixon had thought it would be.

Or my mate's scent is all over the room.

When Dixon walked past a big, strawberry-blond-haired man bussing a table, he finally received his first lungful of the scent directly from the source. His cock went ramrod straight behind his fly. He even felt his nipples bead.

Oh, hot damn, that's good.

Taking in the way the shifter placed the dishes someone had left on the table into a large blue tub, Dixon understood how the scent had ended up everywhere. His mate worked in the cafeteria. With his mate distracted, he took a few seconds to admire the man Fate had deemed the other half of his soul.

The stranger had broad shoulders, a thick neck, and heavily muscled limbs. His biceps stretched the short sleeves of his polo shirt enticingly, and his rather ragged-looking jeans caressed his meaty ass deliciously. Even the obvious pooch and love handles couldn't detract from the man's gorgeous physique.

Dixon wanted to explore every inch of the big shifter's six-foot-four-inch body. With the man topping him by an inch, he figured it would be an adjustment to kiss someone taller than himself, but he would be happy to make it. The plump lips on the man's boy-next-door features begged to be sucked and nibbled.

Finally, the shifter inhaled deeply, and his attention snapped to Dixon. His hazel eyes were wide in his tanned face, and confusion filled them. He furrowed strawberry-blond brows that matched the ear-length tresses on his head.

"Hello, mate," Dixon greeted, figuring it was best to start as he meant to go — straightforward and honest. "Will you tell me your name?"

"Mate?"

The man's deep voice wrapped around Dixon's senses, causing his dick to twitch.

Then the guy shook his head, his hazel eyes twinkling. "Naw. I ain't your mate." Even as he denied their connection, he grinned. "Fate don't pair two dudes. My brother explained it to me." He nodded as if what he was saying was completely accurate. "He told me even though I occasionally think a guy is hot, I can't act on it, because then Fate will never bring me my *real* mate."

"Your brother told you this?" Dixon asked instead of immediately claiming his brother was wrong. That wouldn't win him any points. "When?"

Shrugging massive shoulders, the shifter told him, "Any

time he catches me lookin' at a guy." His face took on a pink-ish hue as he reached down and adjusted the clearly defined erection behind his fly. "He's real smart. Not like me." He broke eye contact and returned to filling his tub. "So, even though you smell real good and my dick is drippin', I can't touch. Then I'll never get a real mate. Sorry."

Dixon's mind reeled as he processed everything the man had rambled. He clearly believed everything his brother had told him to the point of not acknowledging their connection. Before Dixon could come up with a viable counter, the man glanced his way and spoke again.

"Um, anyway. I gotta get back to work."

Then he hustled toward the kitchen.

"Not go as planned?"

Dixon jerked his gaze from the closed door. He'd been star-ing at it long enough that the swinging door had stopped moving. His focus pinned on Manon.

"Afraid not," Dixon replied softly. "Told you it wouldn't." Seeing the second tray Manon held, he turned and tipped his chin toward the table with the others, noticing how they were staring. "Seems I need to ask a few questions about my mate."

My mate, sadly, seemed a bit . . . dim.

That would make it easy for a dominating brother to ma-nipulate.

When they reached the table, Dixon didn't even have to ask.

Vincentius sniffed the air, obviously catching the smell of his arousal. "If you were coming onto Helsinki, it probably won't work." The lion shifter's expression pinched. "He's on probation after being caught with the rogues, working as a guard." Grimacing, Vincentius added, "The only reason he isn't in the dungeons awaiting punishment is because Hel-sinki was doing as his brother, Rian, instructed him."

"Did Rian get into trouble?" Dixon asked curiously.

If Helsinki is already away from Rian's influence, that would help me.

"Sadly, no," Vincentius revealed with a shake of his head. "Rian is a bouncer at a club, and he claims to have heard about a security opening on a councilman's staff and thought of his brother." Holding Dixon's gaze, he shrugged. "Rian wasn't aware of which councilman, but he told his brother about the position anyway and gave Helsinki the contact information to a guy who happened to be a rogue."

"So Helsinki didn't know," Dixon mused softly as he picked up a fried chicken strip. Manon knew him well. As Dixon dipped the end into a tub of honey mustard, he held Vincentius's gaze. "Well, I'm going to need to know everything about Helsinki. He's my mate."

Vincentius's eyes widened. "Well, fuck."

Before popping the meat into his mouth, Dixon winked. "Yeah. I hope to do that soon."

Dixon's still-hard dick twitched at the thought, his body more than on board with that idea.

CHAPTER TWO

Helsinki Akna hurried back into the kitchen. He did his best to ignore his erection—and his bear growling unhappily in his mind—as he placed the tub of dishes on the counter and began unloading them. Taking slow deep breaths, he focused on clearing his lungs of the other shifter's delicious scent.

But, gods, did he smell good!

That thought didn't help. In fact, it made his sex twitch behind his fly.

Want him.

Grimacing, Helsinki did his best to blank his mind, urging his animal to hush and relax. Normally, he could do it easily. He could focus on whatever job Rian had given him, and he would zone out.

Even though Rian didn't like it when Helsinki did that, because his brother had to call his name several times to get his attention, there was no better way to get through cleaning his brother's bathroom.

For someone who was so smart, Rian sure could be a pig.

Well, that's what I'm there for.

Rian had told Helsinki enough times. "I make sure we have a roof over our head and food on the table." He would pin him with a serious expression. "You know you don't know how to save. If I didn't keep part of your paycheck, you'd blow it all on video games and candy." Then Rian would swing his hand to indicate their three-bedroom home. "The least you can do is keep the place tidy, so we have a nice place for me to come home to after taking care of us all day."

Helsinki always nodded, even though he didn't understand why Rian going to work was him taking care of them. After all, Helsinki worked, too. He'd been a part-time bagger at a grocery store.

Well, all that was before, Helsinki realized.

Gods, I'm afraid to think of what the bathroom and kitchen will look like when I'm done with my restitution and move back home.

Rian had told Helsinki to call a guy named Warsaw, who was interested in muscle to protect a councilman. Evidently, Warsaw had told Rian that brains weren't a requirement. As long as the guy followed orders, it didn't matter if he was smart.

His brother had decided Helsinki would fit the bill, and the pay had appeared fantastic. He'd even been able to work around his part-time job hours.

Too good to be true.

Never had an expression been truer, in Helsinki's opinion — not that anyone would ever ask for it. During his second guard assignment, a group of council enforcers had descended on them while they were waiting for . . . someone. Helsinki had shifted and attacked, as he'd been told to do.

Too bad no one had bothered to ask how dominant his bear was . . . because, well, he wasn't. His instincts had him backing down at the first roar of the komodo dragon shifter. Enforcer Dane's animal was damn scary.

After hearing why Helsinki had been there, and he'd answered every question to the best of his ability, the council had been lenient on him. Even though he'd lost his job as a bagger, he didn't need it, since the council required him to stay in a suite at their headquarters. He could even shift when he wanted, as long as he had a guard and remained in certain sections of the fake golf and spa resort that was Shifter Council's headquarters' cover.

"Hey." Desmond nudged Helsinki with his elbow as he

passed him, heading toward a food preparation table.

At first, Helsinki thought the cook was speaking to him because he'd zoned out . . . and not in the way he'd intended. Then he saw Desmond's smile, and confusion filled him.

"Uh, yeah?"

Desmond jerked his chin toward the door that led to the cafeteria. "See someone out there you like?" he asked with an eyebrow waggle.

For a second, Helsinki wasn't certain how to answer that. "Someone I like?"

Then it clicked, and he felt his neck and cheeks flush. He swallowed hard as he glanced down at his still-tented fly. At least embarrassment was getting *that* under control. After he cleared his throat, he forced himself to meet Desmond's gaze again.

Rubbing the back of his neck, Helsinki returned to his task of emptying his dish tub. "Uh, had a hot guy hit on me," he admitted. After all, a shifter could smell lies. Then he hurried to add, "But I turned him down. After all" — Helsinki glanced Desmond's way before finishing — "I wanna meet my mate as much as the next shifter. Can't do somethin' that will piss off Fate, right?"

"Wait. Piss off Fate?" Desmond sounded confused. "What do you mean by that, Hels?"

Placing the last dish on the counter next to where the dishwasher pulled from, Helsinki rolled his shoulders in a shrug. "You know. By acting like a fag."

"Oh, damn," Desmond whispered.

Hearing the surprise in the other shifter's tone caused Helsinki to snap his attention to him. The man's brown eyes were huge in his face, and his cheeks were flushed — except, from the scent the red fox shifter was throwing off, it wasn't embarrassment.

Why do I scent fear?

"Des?"

Did I say something wrong?

Helsinki knew he did that on occasion. Rian told him all the time. His brother had warned him to just keep his fucking mouth shut, so it didn't get him into more trouble.

Did it get me into trouble?

Desmond licked his lips as his brows furrowed. After a quick sniff at the air, he whispered, "Are you bigoted, Hels? I didn't think it of you, but — " Cocking his head, Desmond narrowed his eyes. "Or are you just repeating something you heard?"

Rubbing the back of his neck, Helsinki tried to decide how to answer.

Is this a test? My brother is friends with a lot of people.

Somehow, Rian always knew when he talked about their private at-home conversations with other people. His brother never talked about his views in the open, but he made certain Helsinki followed them . . . one way or another. Helsinki rubbed his shoulder as phantom pain lanced through the back of it.

His brother's bear's claws were sharp.

"Um, just so you know," Desmond began speaking again. "I don't like the word fag." He narrowed his eyes. "And never, *ever* let the mated men on the council hear you use it." Shaking his head, Desmond muttered, "Or even the majority of the enforcers. You'll have your ass handed to you."

Helsinki opened his mouth, then closed it again. "Uh . . . okay." Rubbing the back of his neck again, he tried to reason out the man's words. "Um, no more using the word fag."

That would be hard, but he would manage it. Rian used it every time he talked about fa — *No, homosexuals. Gods, this is gonna be hard.*

Meeting Desmond's gaze, Helsinki muttered, "Um, do you know my brother? Rian?"

Seeing as Rian used the fact that shifters always scented lies to his advantage, Helsinki figured he could do the same.

While he'd never done much more than pass a few words with Desmond in the past, he needed to know what he could or couldn't say in front of him.

Rian's lessons on *don't speak* were more useful than his brother had intended, in Helsinki's opinion.

"Rian?" Desmond cocked his head. "Your brother, Rian?"

Helsinki nodded once.

Desmond shook his head, then scoffed. "No, I don't know him," he told him while twisting his lips into a sneer. "And I don't mean to offend, him bein' your brother and all, but I've heard him talking to you when he meets up for your weekly lunches." The usually relaxed and fun-loving red fox shifter's countenance hardened. "I don't like the way he talks to you." Then Desmond's cheeks turned pink, and his embarrassment flooded the kitchen. "Uh, sorry. I'm sure no one likes to hear someone thinks their brother is an asshole, but—" Grimacing, he turned his attention back to whatever he was supposed to be prepping. "S-Sorry."

"You think my brother's an asshole?"

Helsinki wouldn't have gotten that from Desmond if he hadn't come right out and said it. Of course, he knew he wasn't the most perceptive shifter. Unable to help himself, he moved toward the man and touched his shoulder.

Torn between his curiosity and his desire to defend his brother, Helsinki hesitated. Curiosity won out. "What does Rian say that makes you think he's an asshole?"

Desmond gave Helsinki a look he couldn't decipher. "Weeell." He cleared his throat, then stated, "I heard him tell you to remember to keep your mouth shut, so people don't realize how stupid you are."

Rolling his eyes, Helsinki smirked. "Aww, he's just reminding me not to say stuff that'll piss people off because I don't always think before I speak." He thought he saw concern in the fox shifter's eyes, so he waved a hand toward him as he added, "Like how I said the word fag and you got upset. I didn't mean anythin' by it. I think some guys are hot, too." Realizing what he'd just admitted, he hurried to add, "But since Fate don't mate two dudes, I don't wanna upset her by fuckin' one. He said she won't send me my mate if I do that."

"Who the fuck said that?"

Helsinki turned and spotted Enforcer Delanrue standing inside the doorway. The man's piercing gaze pinned him with a dark stare. His lips were curved into a frown, and his hazel eyes were narrowed.

Fear caused ice to zip through Helsinki's veins. He hunched his shoulders. Somehow, he felt the blood drain from his cheeks, and he knew he paled.

Drawing an enforcer's attention was never a good thing — especially Enforcer Delanrue.

"I-I'm sorry, Enforcer," Helsinki mumbled, dipping his head. Something he'd said must have been wrong, but as he reviewed his comment, he didn't know what it was. "I-I didn't m-mean to offend."

Enforcer Delanrue stalked toward him, his expression grim.

Helsinki shrank back a step, and his bear cowered in the back of his mind.

"I asked" — Enforcer Delanrue grabbed Helsinki's shoulder, but his grip remained surprisingly light even as it held him firmly in place — "who the fuck said that?"

"R-Rian," Helsinki whispered. Not responding just wasn't an option, no matter how pissed his brother was going to be to be put on Enforcer Delanrue's radar.

A low, menacing growl rumbled from the bigger man. Except, when Enforcer Delanrue slid his large hand up Helsinki's neck to grip it, the hold remained loose. He used his thumb under Helsinki's chin to force him to lift his head and meet the enforcer's gaze.

To Helsinki's surprise, Enforcer Delanrue peered at him with concern in his eyes even as a tick twitched in his jaw. "I came to order a rare steak with a loaded baked potato, but there was no one at the window."

"Sorry, Enforcer," Desmond murmured. "It's my fault. I was teasing Helsinki, and our conversation distracted me."

Enforcer Delanrue flicked his gaze to Desmond, but only for an instant, before refocusing on Helsinki. "It's fine, Desmond," he told him. "Now you know, so if you could get it started, I'd appreciate it."

Even Helsinki knew a dismissal when he heard it.

"Yes, Enforcer," Desmond replied before hurrying to obey.

Helsinki heard the tap of Desmond's shoes on the tile floor, but he couldn't tear his gaze away from Enforcer Delanrue's intense stare.

"Is that why you turned away Dixon's attention, Helsinki?"

Parting his lips in surprise, Helsinki felt shock flood him. *Is that his name?* "H-How did you know about—" Heat bloomed in his face as he realized he wasn't answering the dominant enforcer's question. "Y-Yes, Enforcer." Unable to help himself, Helsinki blurted out, "Who else knows?"

If Rian found out a guy hit on Helsinki, even though he'd turned him down, he would be pissed. A shiver of fear worked down his spine upon thinking of the beating his brother would give him.

Rian just doesn't want any of the fag taint associated with our name.

Enforcer Delanrue's nostrils flared, and his eyes narrowed. Even his face flushed just a little. The scent of his anger flooded the air around them.

Helsinki trembled. If he hadn't still been in the enforcer's hold, he would have turned and run. As it was, he barely managed to breathe through his rising panic.

His voice raspy, Enforcer Delanrue rumbled, "You didn't

mean to say that out loud. Did you, Helsinki?"

"S-Say what?" Helsinki managed to squeak out.

"Your comment about fag taint."

Gasping, Helsinki whimpered, "N-No."

Enforcer Delanrue pushed into his space and dipped his head, placing his lips directly near Helsinki's ear. In a gruff rumble, he murmured, "I'm glad I overheard you, Helsinki. Your mate needs to know the trouble coming his way."

"M-My mate?" Helsinki's heart pounded in his chest. "Y-You know, um, know who my m-mate is?"

"So do you, Helsinki," Enforcer Delanrue stated, his voice softening. Lifting his head, he smiled — actually *smiled* — down at him. "Why do you think your bear was pissed when you walked away from Dixon?"

Helsinki felt the hairs on his nape stand on end. Could what Dixon and Enforcer Delanrue was saying be true? "B-But Fate doesn't . . ." Letting his words trail off upon seeing the enforcer's arched brow even as he managed to narrow his eyes. "Does she?"

Enforcer Delanrue nodded. "Indeed, she does." Stepping away, he released him. "Here's my advice, Helsinki, but it's up to you to take it." He crossed his arms over his chest. "Are you listening?"

Nodding, Helsinki clenched and unclenched his fingers, uncertain if he was supposed to say anything.

"Answer me verbally, Helsinki," Enforcer Delanrue ordered, taking away his confusion. "If a shifter of a higher rank asks you a question, you answer verbally. Do you understand?"

Helsinki began nodding again, then quickly murmured, "Yes, Enforcer."

"Good." Cocking his head, Enforcer Delanrue pinned him with a serious expression. "Now then. Here's my advice." He gripped Helsinki's neck, squeezing lightly, as he told him,

"Rian is wrong. Listen to your bear, not your brother's opinion. If your bear wants Dixon, then you need to accept Dixon." Enforcer Delanrue's firm lips quirked into a slight smirk. "You never want to go against your animal, Helsinki."

Nodding slowly, Helsinki thought about his bear's reaction to the other shifter. His animal had perked up in his mind, and he'd wanted to lean down and sniff the man's neck. The other guy—Dixon—had smelled good from a few feet away, making his dick ache, and he'd wanted to lick his flesh to see if he tasted just as fantastic.

His bear had wanted to sink his canines into him and taste his blood.

Just thinking about that caused Helsinki's cock to thicken anew in his jeans.

Enforcer Delanrue chuckled low in his throat, the noise sounding rough.

Holy shit! He does know how to laugh.

With a wink, Enforcer Delanrue released Helsinki and took a step backward. "Your shift is over."

Helsinki glanced at the clock, then refocused on the enforcer, preparing to tell him he had another two hours.

Pointing toward the door that led to the cafeteria, Enforcer Delanrue ordered, "You go now. When a shifter finds his mate, they find concentrating difficult. Go to your room, get cleaned up, and think about what I've told you."

"Yes, Enforcer," Helsinki murmured. After all, what else could he say?

Doing as he'd been bidden, he left the kitchen.

As Helsinki made his way across the cafeteria, he felt the hairs on his nape stand on end. When he glanced around, he spotted Mason—a rhino shifter and one of Rian's friends—watching him. He dipped his head in acknowledgment but kept moving.

Still feeling eyes on him, Helsinki paused as he opened the door. He swept his gaze over the room once more. Meeting

Dixon's gaze, he sucked in a harsh breath.

Helsinki couldn't help but lick his lips upon taking in the feral desire in the depths of those ice-blue eyes. His gut clenched, and his prick sprang back to life. He panted for a moment, shocked upon feeling such a visceral reaction.

His bear roared in his mind, urging him to cross the cafeteria and pull the man into his arms.

Mine! Mate!

Shuddering, Helsinki fought his animal and did as Enforcer Delanrue had instructed. He headed to his room, so he could think about everything that had just happened.

CHAPTER THREE

It took every bit of Dixon's self-control to stay in his seat. His mate had made eye contact before he'd fled. That was something.

He's not immune to me.

Hearing a tap, tap on the table, Dixon snapped his attention away from the closed door. He focused on Jared Templeton, the human mate of his pack's head enforcer — Carson Angeni. As soon as Dixon made eye contact with Jared, the human used a finger to discreetly point to the left.

Dixon followed where the human indicated, and he spotted the sneering visage of a dark-haired stranger. The way the man's attention was fixed on the door Helsinki had just exited caused the hairs on his nape to stand on end. Then the guy turned his head and focused on Dixon.

Holding the other shifter's gaze, Dixon refused to look away. He had no clue who the man was, but he had zero intention of giving him any indication of submission. While supposing he could be an enforcer, which would make his station on par with Dixon's own, the snarl in his wolf's mind told him otherwise.

To Dixon's satisfaction, the other guy looked away — after showing off one canine, first.

Whatever.

Turning back to his food, Dixon speared a bite of sausage link. As he brought it to his mouth, he realized he held Regales's attention. Before popping the food into his mouth, Dixon asked, "Did I just insult an enforcer?"

Dixon figured he should just toss the idea out there.

Regales shook his head. "No. That's Mason Rutner. He's a tracker for the council."

"And not a very good one," Enforcer Delanrue announced, joining them. "He's under review."

"Really?" Regales slathered blackberry jam onto a piece of English muffin. "Why?"

Delanrue snorted before glancing over his shoulder at Mason.

Dixon followed his gaze.

The shifter in question was rising to his feet, tossing a used napkin onto his plate. He walked toward the doors while pulling out his cell phone, not even bothering to take his dishes to the drop off zone.

What an ass.

"On his last assignment, it took him two weeks to locate the shifter in question when it really should have only taken him two days," Delanrue revealed, refocusing on his food. "He's also associated with Rian."

"Helsinki's brother?" Dixon clarified.

"The same." Delanrue took a bite of his loaded baked potato, then talked around his food. "There's been other shit, too." Smirking, he stared at Regales while muttering, "Like two decades ago, he was hired by Krakow."

Regales's eyes narrowed. "Why wasn't he cleared out with all the other riff-raff connected with the rogues?"

Dixon sure appreciated that Regales's growling voice wasn't directed at him. Sure, he was a dominant son-of-a-bitch, but he was a wolf. His animal didn't cower in his mind, but it sure kept a wary eye on the big grizzly councilman.

Delanrue didn't seem fazed, however. While rolling one shoulder in a half-shrug, he swallowed his mouthful. As Delanrue scooped up a forkful of steak, he replied, "He was never on any of the lists Nkosi sent us." Before popping the bite into his mouth, he added, "It wasn't until we were look-ing into Helsinki and Rian and connected Mason to Hels' older brother and looked into him that we stumbled over the information."

"That doesn't explain the sneers," Dixon commented idly, thinking of the dirty looks Mason gave not only the door after Helsinki had exited but himself. "Especially to a complete stranger."

Pausing, Delanrue set down his fork with a sigh. "After overhearing a comment Helsinki made in the kitchen, some-thing his brother told him, I figure Mason is a bigot, too." He wiped his hands on a napkin before grabbing the bowl of blackberry jam on the table. "Especially since he was hired by that asshole Krakow. Birds of a feather and all that shit."

"What did Helsinki say?" Dixon asked.

As Delanrue shared what had happened in the kitchen, Dixon forced himself to keep eating. He was hungry, after all, and it took plenty of energy to shift and run. If he intended to put his plans into motion, he needed sustenance.

Of course, as Dixon heard the lies Rian had been filling Hel-sinki's head with, his gut churned and he had to swallow sev-eral times to keep down his food.

Well, damn.

Then Delanrue shared his words of wisdom to Helsinki.

Huh. The dude's deeper than I thought.

Never would Dixon share that thought, however. He never wanted to be on the massive enforcer's bad side.

"Then I'll finish my food and put my plan into action," Dixon claimed. Pausing with his fork halfway to his mouth, he glanced between the two bear shifters at the table. "If you both are still game?"

"Of course," Alpha Kontra replied. His smile appeared a little feral, and his deep brown eyes even seemed to gleam. "I'm always up for de-bunking bigoted propaganda."

"Me, too," Regales confirmed.

Jared chuckled huskily. "I just like kicking the bigoted ass's . . . ass." He waggled his eyebrows playfully.

"What's your plans?" Delanrue questioned before sinking his teeth into a jam-covered roll.

"While you explain my plan, I'm going to go invite Helsinki," Dixon told everyone. He'd managed to get through two-thirds of his meal, but his wolf was riding him hard to track down their confused mate. "What's his room number?"

After getting the information from Regales, as well as instructions on how to get there, Dixon placed his dirty dishes on the platter Manon had used to carry their food to the table. He noticed the Cajun enforcer and Jared putting their own silverware on their plates. When they both moved the dishes to the platter, too, Dixon glanced between them.

"You know, you don't have to join me," Dixon told them. He waved his hand in an absent manner. "We *are* in the Shifter Council building."

Scoffing, Jared replied, "And we just learned there are still bigoted assholes here."

Dixon rolled his eyes. "They're everywhere, Jared."

"Except, it's kind of our jobs while we're here, Beta," Manon pointed out as he rose to his feet. "We'll stay around the corner or something, letting you have a bit of privacy to ask out your mate."

Jared sighed, the noise sounding put-upon. "Then how am I supposed to offer advice if it seems he's going to turn you down?"

While picking up the tray, Dixon bit back a groan. "I think I can handle it," he claimed dryly as he headed toward the drop-off counter.

"But if we told Helsinki about how fantastic sex with your mate is, I'm sure he would—"

When Jared's voice suddenly cut off, Dixon glanced over his shoulder. He smirked.

Manon had one hand on Jared's shoulder and the second over the human's mouth. "Zee man seemed shy enough, Jared," the enforcer murmured, lowering his hand. "Let zem connect first, *oui?*"

Jared smirked. "Very well." Crossing his arms over his chest, he added with a grin, "But know I'm happy to help."

Dixon placed the trash in the bin as a low chuckle escaped him. "I'll keep that in mind." After setting the dishes in the indicated area, he headed toward the door, the pair flanking him.

Following Regales's directions, Dixon found the wing which housed those working on-site. From the space between doors, he figured each one would be set up as a decent-sized one-bedroom apartment. The walls were tastefully decorated with nature scenes, and the light-brown carpet runner beneath his feet nearly blended into the wood flooring.

Easily finding Helsinki's apartment number, Dixon paused before it. He lifted his hand to knock, then paused. Focusing on Jared, he arched one brow in a silent order.

Jared offered him a cheeky smile before turning and heading away from him. He stopped near Manon, who stood twenty-five feet away, leaning against the wall.

Dixon turned his attention back to the door and knocked. Inhaling deeply in an attempt to settle his nerves, he instead caught the faint scent of his mate. His blood heated and flowed south, and his mouth began to water.

Mate. Mine!

Yeah, he's our mate. Dixon mentally agreed with his wolf.

Claim!

Waiting impatiently, Dixon urged his animal to calm down. *We need to coax him.* There was no way they could pounce immediately, no matter how much both halves of him wanted to. *He's been confused.*

Just as Dixon felt his wolf huff in annoyance, he heard the

tumblers of the door lock rumble. He flexed his fingers, anticipation running through him. His urge to grab the man as soon as he appeared and drag him to the nearest bed was almost overwhelming.

Wow! Damn mating urges hit fast.

When the door opened a few inches, Dixon met Helsinki's hazel eyes, which widened in obvious surprise. He watched Helsinki's boy-next-door features morph into uncertainty. When his lips parted and he slid his tongue out to wet his lower one, Dixon wanted to trace that path with his own.

"Hello, Helsinki," Dixon greeted softly, managing to find his tongue. "I'd like the chance to talk to you about what your brother told you."

Helsinki nibbled his bottom lip, then opened the door wider. Except, he didn't invite Dixon inside. Instead, he lifted his cell to his ear and stated, "Um, sorry, Ri. I'm gonna have to call you back."

With Dixon's increased shifter hearing, he easily made out the other side of the conversation.

"Don't you dare hang up on me, Helsinki," a deep voice—Rian—demanded. "You better not be doin' somethin' to embarrass me. You know how I feel about that."

There was a distinct growl in the brother's voice, and Dixon fought the urge to grab the phone and tell the guy off by gritting his teeth. He clenched his fists for a heartbeat, then two. Seeing Helsinki's face flush and scenting his unease mixed with embarrassment, Dixon forced his own ire to ease.

Don't want to add to my mate's upset.

"I ain't gonna do nothin' to embarrass ya," Helsinki mumbled, a frown tipping his lips. "Look. Someone's at my door. I gotta go."

Rian huffed a sigh. "It's probably Mason. He said he'd check in on you."

Oh, hell, no.

From the grimace that flicked across Helsinki's features—

there and gone so fast that Dixon almost missed it—he figured his mate didn't want to see that shifter any more than Dixon wanted him near his mate.

"Right," Helsinki rumbled un-committedly. "Well, later."

As Helsinki began to lower the phone, obviously intent on disconnecting, Rian called out, "Finish your time there, bro. The bathroom's lookin' a little rough."

Helsinki rolled his eyes and disconnected without responding.

Huh.

Dixon waited and watched as Helsinki took a ragged breath, then a second one. Finally, his mate refocused on him, meeting his gaze. A muscle ticked in his square jaw even as his nostrils flared and a pinkish hue climbed up his neck.

The unmistakable scent of arousal wafted through the air, and Dixon's body answered. His cock ached behind his fly, and pre-cum oozed from him. He began to lift his arm, wanting to touch Helsinki, but the slight stiffening of his posture stayed Dixon's hand.

Placing his hand on the doorframe instead, Dixon murmured, "I know this place has a designated area for you to shift around here, but I thought you might like to go somewhere else to stretch your bear's legs." He kept his voice smooth and soothing. "After letting our animals out, we could shift and talk about this connection between us."

Rubbing the back of his neck with his free hand, Helsinki mumbled, "I can't go for runs anywhere but here."

"Unless you're accompanied by a couple of approved members working for the council," Dixon countered, offering a smile. "Which I have arranged."

"Really?" Helsinki looked confused.

Dixon cocked his head. "You didn't know someone could take you running?"

Helsinki shook his head. "Rian explained the rules to me. He said I could only shift at one location around here."

"Of course he did," Dixon grumbled, hating the control Rian seemed to be exerting over his mate. Seeing Helsinki's brows furrow, he forced a lightness to his tone. "Do you have a copy of your contract with the Shifter Council? The one you signed that outlined your duties as you worked off your penance?"

Shaking his head again, Helsinki stated, "Rian's keeping it safe for me at home."

Resisting the urge to grit his teeth, Dixon nodded instead. "Well, one of the people we'll be running with is Councilman Regales." He smiled upon seeing Helsinki's clearly surprised expression. "I'm certain he wouldn't be hanging with us if what we were doing was against the rules."

"Really?" Helsinki slowly began to smile. "Councilman Regales is a bear, too. It'd be fun to run with another bear." Then his expression faded to one of concern. "But he's a grizzly. My brother said—"

Dixon couldn't help himself. He was tired of hearing about what Rian said. Reaching out, he touched his fingertips to Helsinki's lips.

To his pleasure, his mate froze . . . except for the gasp and slight tremble of his lips.

"I know you're confused, Helsinki, but you are my mate," Dixon murmured, doing his best to sound encouraging. "I would never do anything that would put you at risk or get you in trouble." Easing a step closer, he slid his hand from Helsinki's mouth, so he could cradle his bear's jaw. "I've already arranged it with the councilman. We'll also be meeting Alpha Kontra, who's also a grizzly bear. If you're concerned about a polar bear running with grizzlies, a guy named Hess will be coming, too. He's a Kodiak bear shifter."

Helsinki stared at him with wide eyes, his breathing appearing to come in short, soft pants.

Dixon relished the reactions of his mate. While he wanted

to seal his lips over Helsinki's mouth so badly, he knew that now wasn't the time or place. Still, he couldn't resist rubbing the pad of his thumb under his bottom lip, feeling the plump flesh.

"Your contract requires two council representatives," Dixon continued, unable to help how raspy his voice had become. "So the other will be Enforcer Dane Drudeson."

For a long moment, they just stared at each other. Dixon took in the dilation of Helsinki's eyes, seeing the brown dominate the green. His mate's lips were parted, and he even flicked out his tongue, touching it to the pad of Dixon's thumb.

Groaning ever-so-softly, Dixon urged, "Please, come, Helsinki."

"O-Okay." Helsinki swallowed so hard his Adam's apple bobbed. "Wh-When?"

"Right now."

The sound of Manon clearing his throat drew Dixon's attention. Tearing his gaze away from his mate, he turned his head. Upon seeing Mason striding their way, he bit back a low growl.

Dixon turned back to Helsinki and met his gaze. "My pack-mates are waiting. Manon is the shifter, and Jared is the human." With one more brush to his jaw, he lowered his hand. "Grab your wallet. It's time to go."

Helsinki nodded and pushed his phone into his front pocket. Then he grabbed his wallet off the side table and shoved it into a back one. Finally, he snagged a set of keys and stepped out of his apartment, Dixon backing up to give him room.

While Helsinki locked up, Dixon noted the way Manon and Jared joined him, placing themselves between him, his mate, and an angry-expressioned Mason.

When Helsinki turned, he froze. "Oh, um." His tone gave

away his unease just as much as his scent did. "Hey, Mason."

Dixon did not like the way Helsinki hunched his shoulders . . . as if he were waiting to be chastised — or struck.

Oh, fuck. No more.

CHAPTER FOUR

Tension rocketed through Helsinki's body along with a healthy dose of embarrassment.

Why did Mason have to walk up now?

Helsinki's bear rumbled in his mind, urging him to get closer to Dixon.

Protect mate.

While a bit of confusion filled him, Helsinki did as his beast wanted. He would protect his mate from Rian's friend.

Oh. I already think of him as my mate?

Mine!

While Helsinki still felt a wealth of confusion about the whole thing, he knew his bear had made up his mind.

"Come on, Helsinki," Mason demanded, beckoning. "Move away from those guys, and let's head back into your rooms." He pointed at the door Helsinki had just locked. "We need to call your brother."

That was the last thing Helsinki wanted to do. Still, he'd always obeyed Mason in the past. His body moved right, instinctively doing the other shifter's bidding.

Dixon rested his hand on Helsinki's hip, gripping him gently and staying his movement. Heat bloomed from the wolf shifter's touch. His gut clenched a little, and his dick, which had softened upon seeing Mason, began to thicken anew.

His hand feels good on me. What would it be like to have it on my bare skin?

Before Helsinki could get too lost in those thoughts, Dixon stated, "Helsinki is going for a run with us." He squeezed lightly. "He'll have to catch up with you another time."

"You can run with others later," Mason stated, his focus still on Helsinki, not acknowledging Dixon. He began reaching toward his arm. "Come on."

Helsinki recognized the snub and frowned. He knew he wasn't the sharpest tool in the shed, but even he realized that wasn't a smart move. Due to Helsinki's bear being fairly laid-back and non-aggressive, he'd easily recognized Dixon's dominance.

"Do not ignore me, Tracker Mason Rutner," Dixon growled the words, stepping between Helsinki and Mason. The move caused the rhino shifter's hand to touch Dixon's chest instead of Helsinki, and he batted the other shifter's hand away. "And do not order Helsinki around. He doesn't answer to you."

Clenching his hands into fists, Mason snapped, "I don't know who you think you are, but back off, dog." His lips curled, and he narrowed his dark eyes as he took a threatening step forward. "You don't wanna cross me. I work for the council."

"*Oui*, it's clear to see you don't know who this is." Manon stepped into Mason's space, forcing him back a step. "This is Beta Dixon Holsteen of the Stone Ridge wolf pack. You'll give him respect." Upon seeing Mason's eyes widen, Manon smirked. "Oh, seems you've heard of him."

"Fucking faggot pack," Mason snarled, curling his lip. Disgust dripped from his tone. "You should be disbanded and your kind put down."

Jared tsked. "Now, now." His tone sounded, well, not jovial. Maybe entertained, Helsinki decided — which he found odd — as the human continued, "Slurring homosexual pairings might just get you into trouble, foolish shifter." Smirking, Jared snickered, but the noise seemed anything but amused. "After all, several on the council have completed fated bonds with men."

Mason narrowed his eyes, and he took a step forward again. Except, Manon's confident posturing caused him to step backward once more. Still, he managed to bark a hoarse laugh.

"Fate don't mate two men"—after a second, Mason added—"or two women, together. You're abominations, and she'll never grant you a bond."

"And *that* is the backward kind of thinking that will *really* drive Fate to forsake you," Dixon stated as he tightened his grip on Helsinki's waist and hip. Confidently using his hold to turn Helsinki toward the bank of elevators, he ordered, "Don't make me report your threats against the Stone Ridge pack to the council, Mason." Then Dixon paused and pinned a cold look on the rhino shifter. "Of course, since our pack likes to take out threats to us ourselves, I really hope you don't listen to me."

"You son-of-a-bitch!" Mason screamed, but he didn't pursue them. "You'll wish you never tried to come between brothers."

Jared snorted as he called over his shoulder, "Looking forward to seeing what you come up with." Pausing an instant, he waggled his brows in an obvious taunt. "We've certainly taken down those far more intimidating than you."

Roaring, Mason finally lunged, aiming at the human. Helsinki's bear rumbled uncertainly in his mind. He realized he actually had an inkling need to protect another from Mason, and he couldn't remember the last time he'd felt an urge to go against the rhino shifter.

Have I ever?

To Helsinki's surprise, neither of the wolf shifters moved to protect Jared. A second later, Helsinki realized why. The human spun to the left, grabbed Mason's outstretched arm, and used his momentum to slam the rhino shifter face-first into the wall.

Mason had just enough presence of mind to bring up his other hand, keeping himself from getting a broken nose.

Jared had somehow managed to wrench Mason's arm behind his back. With a hand on the rhino shifter's wrist, he yanked up high, almost to his neck. He pressed a knife he'd pulled from . . . somewhere . . . against Mason's side.

Leaning close, Jared stated, "You assume too much, Mason."

"But you're human." Even with the anger filtering through Mason's tone, he still sounded shocked.

"I am," Jared confirmed. Chuckling, he told him, "You know those pesky rumors about how humans bonded with a shifter gain a measure of increased strength, speed, and resilience." Leaning close, Jared purred into Mason's ear, "Well, they're true. I'm the mate of Carson Angeni, a wolf shifter." Then his voice took on an amused quality. "Although, even without the perks of bonding, I still would have been able to incapacitate you. Your tells completely give you away."

Mason growled, jerking in Jared's hold. He hissed and stilled, probably due to the knife the human still held against his ribs. The acrid scent of iron confirmed Helsinki's guess.

"If you weren't carrying that knife, I'd —" Mason began.

"*Zut alors,*" Manon grumbled, interrupting the rhino shifter. "Just shut it, Mason. Move on, or we'll call for security."

A mutinous expression flicked across Mason's face, but then it cleared. Hate filled his dark eyes even as he dipped his chin in a slight nod.

Manon tapped Jared's shoulder. As Jared released Mason and stepped away, the wolf enforcer kept a sharp eye on the other shifter. He watched him with narrowed eyes as Mason turned and stalked down the hallway, pulling his phone out in the process.

Helsinki instinctively knew who Mason was calling. As

Dixon guided him into an elevator car, he couldn't help the tension thrumming through his body. He hadn't gone against Rian and his buddies in a long, *long* time, but he remembered some of the *lessons* they'd given him to help *straighten him out.*

"Will you tell me what you're thinking about, Hels?" Dixon asked softly as the elevator stopped on the main floor, and they stepped out.

"Rian ain't gonna be happy when he hears about me goin' with you," Helsinki admitted, glancing up and down the hall uneasily. He half expected Rian to appear around the corner. "He don't like fags." Remembering Desmond's words in the kitchen, Helsinki felt his cheeks heat. He glanced between the guys with him and quickly amended, "Um, I-I mean gays."

Sighing, Dixon guided him toward the parking garage. "I sort of figured that out, handsome."

Dixon's full lips curved into a smile that enticed Helsinki, making him want to reach out and touch.

Would the dominant shifter mind?

Rian sure would have.

Helsinki grimaced, hating that he was comparing Dixon to his brother.

"Hey, what are you thinking that put that expression on your face?" Dixon stopped and gripped Helsinki's upper arm, but it wasn't a tight hold. Instead, it felt reassuring. "Whatever it is, you can tell me, my mate."

Helsinki hesitated, his gaze flicking from Dixon's face to that of the other men. Manon was busy opening the door to the parking garage, then visually checking out the area. Jared, on the other hand, peered down the hallway in the direction they'd come, as if watching for pursuit.

Taking a chance—after all, if Dixon did end up responding similar to Rian, Helsinki needed to know as soon as possible—he admitted, "I got distracted looking at your lips." After a quick swallow, he continued, "You have thick lips, and I wondered if you'd let me touch them."

To Helsinki's surprise, Dixon grinned broadly. "You can touch them anytime you want."

Shocked, Helsinki barked, "Really?"

"Mmm-hmmm," Dixon confirmed, his blue eyes holding a warmth Helsinki had never expected to have directed his way. Then Dixon cocked his head as he sobered. "So why the grimace?"

Recalling his thoughts, Helsinki sighed deeply. "After wondering if I could touch your lips, I realized that no way would Rian ever want another guy to touch his lips. I was wondering, um —" He scratched the back of his neck, thinking hard as he mumbled, "How do I say this without bein' rude?"

Dixon squeezed Helsinki's arm. "You don't have to explain, if you don't want to, Hels." With a twitch of his lips, he added, "Or I could guess." Then Dixon pointed toward where Manon beckoned. "Come on."

As they walked through the parking garage, Dixon slid his hand to the small of Helsinki's back.

A shiver worked through Helsinki, and his breath caught in his throat. As Dixon teased his thumb over his fabric-covered spine, a zing traveled up and around him. The hairs on his nape stood on end while his prick twitched behind his fly.

"Wow," Helsinki muttered, more to himself than anyone around him. "If that little touch makes my dick swell, I wonder what your hand actually on my skin would make it do."

Dixon chuckled, the sound husky. His fingers twitched along Helsinki's spine. "Oh, my mate," he murmured. "I sure hope that's an invitation to find out later."

Helsinki's jaw sagged open, and he snapped his focus to Dixon's face. His eyes widened as he took in the hungry gleam in the wolf shifter's deep blue eyes. He believed he could actually see the other man's desire for him in their depths.

"Oh, wow," Helsinki whispered, a shudder working through his body. "Y-You're, uh, serious."

Blinking once, twice, Dixon took in a deep breath. Holding Helsinki's gaze, he rumbled, "I am, Helsinki. Very much so." He turned his attention to where they were going and pointed off to the left. "Here's our ride."

Upon seeing who waited, Helsinki nearly missed a step. He spotted a black SUV, but it was who stood around it that surprised him. Three men waited.

"W-We're riding with Councilman Regales and his mate?" Helsinki murmured, glancing at Dixon before returning his focus to the group. "Even with Enforcer Dane there, why would they trust me with them?"

Dixon rubbed a palm up and down Helsinki's spine, and he found it soothing. Even his bear relaxed in his mind as if pushing into the touch. He sighed and eased closer to the other shifter.

Smiling, Dixon leaned close and told him, "That's exactly why, Helsinki."

Helsinki figured his confusion must have shown on his face, for Dixon continued with, "You're not an aggressive bear, my mate." His smile appeared wry. "It's why you go along with whatever other people order you to do, but we're going to have to work on that."

Even though Helsinki was still confused, he nodded anyway.

Dixon urged Helsinki to start walking again—he wasn't certain when he'd stopped.

As they approached the trio, Enforcer Dane grinned broadly at them. "So, a run, huh?" He rested his hands on his hips and rolled his neck on his shoulders. "My dragon would be happy to get out for a while. I know the perfect place."

Helsinki didn't trust himself to say anything that wouldn't get him into trouble, so he just nodded.

"Good to see you outside the cafeteria, Helsinki," Regales said by way of greeting. "Is everyone treating you okay?"

As Regales had asked the question, he'd helped his human mate, Theo, into the back of the SUV limo. Then he followed the man inside. The pair sat on the back bench seat.

Knowing a response was required, Helsinki used the time it took to climb into the big vehicle to sort through a viable response. Most of the time, everyone and everything was fine. It was only around certain people — when Rian's friends were around more liberal-minded shifters — that Helsinki grew uncomfortable because he didn't want to upset . . . well, anyone.

Once Helsinki settled on the left side bench seat, Dixon relaxed next to him. He couldn't help but glance down when he felt the other shifter's thigh pressed against his own. Warmth flooded him, seeping up from where they touched and through his body.

The simple contact felt . . . really nice.

Jared and Manon didn't join them, and Helsinki absently wondered where they'd gone. Instead, Dane sat on the bench seat across from them. Glancing toward the front, Helsinki noticed Dane's younger brother, Dakota, sitting behind the wheel.

Dixon placed his hand on Helsinki's thigh and squeezed lightly. "Regales asked you a question," he reminded gently. "Is everything okay at council headquarters?"

Helsinki quickly nodded. "Oh, yeah. Everything's fine." Smiling absently, he shrugged. "I stay in my room most of the time because Rian doesn't want me to accidentally say something stupid that will be an embarrassment to our family name." Upon seeing the looks of concern passed between those in the vehicle with him, Helsinki rubbed at his thigh in discomfort. "I-I just, well —"

"Relax, Helsinki," Dixon urged, rubbing the thigh he still touched. "There is no wrong answer. The truth is always best, even when it reveals a problem that needs to be dealt with."

Helsinki sucked in a harsh breath. "I-I'm a problem?"

"No, Helsinki," Regales quickly assured him. "Your brother's bigoted ideology is the problem."

Frowning, Helsinki mumbled, "Ideology." He met Dixon's gaze, but he couldn't get himself to admit that he didn't know what that meant.

Dixon must have known. "His ideas and opinions on how Fate doesn't pair same-sex couples as well as his way of using his words, fists, and claws to make you behave a certain way."

Helsinki nodded again even as he scowled at the floor of the now-moving vehicle. "How'd you know he did that?"

He felt his face heat, uncomfortable with being the recipient of so many pairs of eyes.

When Dixon cupped his jaw and urged him to meet his gaze, Helsinki sucked in a surprised gasp at the feel of the goose bumps that broke out on his neck in response to the simple contact.

"The way your brother's friend tried to keep us apart told me," Dixon began slowly. "There was anger and hate in his eyes, and I have no doubt, if you'd been alone with him, he would have hit you." Arching one blond brow, he asked, "Can you truthfully tell me I'm wrong?"

Helsinki shook his head just enough to answer because he didn't want to dislodge the wolf shifter's touch to his face. Taking a chance, he admitted something he'd never voiced before. "No. They sure were pissed that my new guard job drew attention to them and their activities."

"Activities?" Dane asked, leaning forward. "What activities? What are they doing?"

Oh shit!

CHAPTER FIVE

The tension that lashed through Helsinki's body—felt through his grip on his thigh—told Dixon that his man hadn't realized his comment would draw questions.

"Relax, Hels," Dixon rumbled, rubbing over his mate's thick thigh. "If they're trying to hide something from the council, it could be dangerous to our kind." Sliding the pad of his thumb along the stubble of his mate's jaw, he urged the man to focus on him. "If they're doing something wrong, it doesn't mean you are."

Helsinki heaved a low sigh as he nuzzled his cheek into Dixon's hold. "He's my brother. My only family."

Dixon wondered if Helsinki even realized he did it or if it was all instinctual.

"And we always want to think well of our family, to take care of them as best as we can," Dixon conceded, thinking of his younger brother who'd been lost to him when the shifter had made his own mistakes. Pushing those thoughts aside, he reminded Helsinki, "But sometimes they screw up, and they need to be held accountable so they can learn from their mistakes and become better people."

Too bad I hadn't realized that decades before with Reagan.

Oh, well. At least, I can try to help my mate by not repeating mine and my parents' mistakes.

Dixon held Helsinki's gaze as he peered into the other shifter's deep hazel eyes. Reading the inner struggle reflected in their depths, he waited patiently. To his relief, no one else spoke, either—the rumble of the tires on pavement the only sounds to fill the space.

"Well, every Thursday night, Rian comes back with bruised knuckles," Helsinki began slowly. His expression turned vacant as he added, "I asked him a couple of times how it'd happened, but he always told me not to worry about it. When I persisted, he—" Helsinki swallowed hard enough to cause his Adam's apple to bob, and he lifted his hand to rub the jaw Dixon wasn't cupping.

To Dixon, the move was very telling.

Helsinki's next words confirmed Dixon's fear.

"Rian cracked my jaw, slamming me into the wall." Pulling away, Helsinki hunched his shoulders and stared at the floor of the vehicle. "I got curious, though. Two weeks later, I followed him when he left the house with Mason and Tanner."

When Helsinki darted his gaze around the vehicle, Dixon realized he needed a little encouragement. "Whatever you say right now, you won't be in trouble," he assured, sliding his left arm around Helsinki's shoulders. He couldn't help but offer his upset mate the comfort of his touch. Leaning close, Dixon murmured into Helsinki's ear. "And I happen to think curiosity is a good thing . . . when in healthy doses."

Helsinki clenched his hands together in his lap even as he peered at Dixon with wide eyes. "Really?"

Dixon wanted to kiss Helsinki so very badly, but he knew this wasn't the time or place for their first. "Indeed, I do," he confirmed instead, nodding once. "I love exploring new scents in the forest or learning about the hobbies and interests of other pack-members." Grinning, deciding to reveal something of himself, Dixon added, "I love horseback riding, and while I'm pretty damn good in the hunter-jumper ring, I made the mistake of thinking that would easily transfer to foxhunting." Laughing at the memory, Dixon shook his head. "Galloping through the countryside chasing a pack of hounds after a fox is completely different than riding a horse around an arena and jumping over obstacles in a specific pattern."

Furrowing his brows, Helsinki muttered, "What's foxhunting?"

While Dixon was surprised at Helsinki's lack of knowledge, he did his best not to bat an eyelash. After all, he liked that his mate felt comfortable asking him questions. "Have you ever seen a picture of a group of men on horseback, normally wearing red jackets, galloping along behind a bunch of hound dogs?"

Hesitating, Helsinki gave off the impression that he was thinking deeply.

"Like this." Dane held out his phone, showing a picture on the screen.

Helsinki's dark eyes lit up, and a wide smile curved his lips as he nodded. "Yeah, I've seen pictures like that." Casting a concerned look Dixon's way, he pointed out, "Those guys are jumping logs and following dogs. You did that? That seems dangerous. Why—" Then Helsinki snapped his mouth shut, cutting off his rambling. Before Dixon could come up with a reply, his mate muttered, "Hunter-jumper. Riding a horse around an arena and . . . oh." Gaping at Dixon, he mumbled, "You do *that* on a horse?"

"Sure do," Dixon confirmed. While he was pleased to see the awe in Helsinki's eyes, he didn't care for the fear there. Deciding to see if he could put his man's mind at ease, he asked, "Do you know how to ride? If not, there are some great lesson horses at the stable where I board my gelding."

Dixon had always loved the idea of having his horse at his place in the mountains. Too bad the logistics had never worked. Between his hours as a park ranger and his duties as the pack beta, he remained pretty busy. His horse—Galahad—received more attention at the facility where Dixon boarded him than what he could ever give him. Plus, even though his two-acre plot had a small barn and paddock, his place didn't have the facilities needed for training—indoor and outdoor arenas, round pens, indoor and outdoor jump obstacles, as well as an extensive trail system.

When the wolf shifter Leonard—Leo to his friends—had bought the dilapidated ranch in the mountains for his human mate, Jerry, the whole pack had worked together to make the place an upscale facility. They'd done it, too. While the pack had worked on that, Jerry had taken online business courses. Even before they'd finished, Jerry had started putting his lessons to work and had begun garnering a clientele.

These days, Jerry and Leo's place was the most successful horse training and boarding facility in the area, despite its remote location halfway between Stone Ridge and Colin City.

"Y-You think . . . uh—" Helsinki looked genuinely confused. "You actually think I could learn to ride a horse?"

"Of course," Dixon immediately replied, giving his bear a reassuring smile. "I know you're a big guy"—he waggled his brows playfully as he swept his gaze over his mate's large frame before meeting his gaze again, pleased to see the slight blush staining his cheeks—"but I can think of at least two of Jerry's lesson horses that could accommodate you."

Helsinki swallowed so hard his Adam's apple bobbed. Watching his mate nibble his bottom lip, Dixon wanted to lean forward and do the same. Only realizing the bear seemed to be in deep thought stayed his natural urge.

"Y-You, uh—" Helsinki paused and cleared his throat before meeting Dixon's gaze through his lashes. "You wouldn't mind me learning new things?"

Well, fuck a duck. Rian has to be the all-time most controlling bastard . . . ever.

Dixon pasted on his most reassuring smile and kept his tone soothing. "Handsome, I will support you in learning anything you want to." Squeezing his mate's opposite shoulder, since he still had his arm slung around him. "Skiing, snowboarding, mountain biking, hang gliding"—Dixon began spouting off some of the more popular stuff tourists came to do near their mountain home—"horseback riding, camping. You wanna learn. I'll be right there either learning beside you or teaching you or whatever you need." Smirking, Dixon added, "Hell, maybe you wanna go to culinary school to be a chef or a baker. You could do that, too."

To Dixon's amusement, Helsinki wrinkled his nose. "Rian always makes me cook for him. I don't mind it, but I don't think I'd wanna—" Helsinki snapped his mouth shut, his lips twisting in a grimace.

Chuckling, Dixon nodded. "Alright," he drawled. "So that's not your thing." He winked. "That's okay. I don't mind cookin'."

Helsinki began to smile as he shook his head.

Unfortunately, Dane broke into the moment. "Sorry to interrupt. Really, I am." The council enforcer scrubbed a hand through his shaggy, dirty-blond hair and twisted his lips into a wry smile. "But we really need to know where Rian is going on Thursday nights. Do you know?"

"Oh, yeah!" Helsinki's brows shot up as his cheeks took on a pinkish hue, meeting the enforcer's brown-eyed gaze. "I followed him one night, and he and his buddies went into this old warehouse." Sighing, he told them, "They were welcomed by the guy at the door with a grin and a backslap. When I tried to walk in, he looked me up and down and asked if I was there to try out." Helsinki's brows furrowed as he admitted, "I didn't know what he meant, so I said no. The guy said I had to go in the front like everybody else. I didn't have enough money, so I had to sneak in." His cheeks darkened to a ruddy glow. "Just 'cause I'm big don't mean I ain't agile. I climbed up the side of the warehouse and snuck in through a third-story window. Hiding in the rafters, I watched what was goin' on."

Helsinki hesitated, then claimed, "I watched Rian beatin'

on some human." Frowning, he glanced around the vehicle. "I mean, hittin' me is one thing. I'm a big bear shifter. I can take it." Appearing completely confused, Helsinki shook his head. "But this was just some human. No way would that ever be a fair fight." Once again, Helsinki hunched his shoulders and stared at the floor. "I asked him about it when he got home. Shoulda kept my big mouth shut."

With the way Helsinki trailed his words off on a whisper, Dixon feared what would come out of his mate's mouth next.

Finally, Helsinki cleared his throat and muttered, "Rian taught me a lesson for questioning his decisions." He wrung his fingers, his knuckles whitening from the pressure. "I couldn't go to work for three days. My boss was pissed, but at least I didn't lose my job." Then a scowl crossed his features. "I have now, though."

"You won't need it in Stone Ridge." The words were out of Dixon's mouth before he could think better of them. Seeing Helsinki's head snap up and his dark eyes wide in obvious shock, he quirked a reassuring smile. "We can find you a new job once there, if that's what you want. Otherwise, you can explore the area and your interests. Maybe take some time to figure out what you want to do when you grow up."

Helsinki cocked his head. "Uh, I'm already grown up."

Dixon waggled his brows as he swept his gaze over Helsinki's big frame, twisting his expression into one of lascivious appreciation. "Oh, my mate," he rumbled huskily, once again peering into Helsinki's wide brown eyes. "I know you're grown up. It was an expression."

"Huh." Helsinki shrugged his shoulders, obviously not completely following. "Okay."

When Dixon felt the car slow, he snapped his attention to the window. Dakota was turning the vehicle onto a long drive. There were trees on either side, and they appeared to be winding their way through a wooded area.

"Where are we?" Dixon asked absently. He would be the first to admit he had never been to Georgia, and he wasn't familiar with anywhere in the state.

"This area is privately owned by Councilman Aiden Ridgeston." It was Dakota who answered from up front. "He allows other councilmen and their guests, as well as some of his friends, to run on his property." Grinning, his expression visible in the rearview mirror. "I've been here a few times. It's gorgeous."

"It looks it," Helsinki commented, his focus riveted to the windows as they passed large oaks, palmettos, and even some mulberries. "He must be rich to own a place like this."

While Dixon exchanged a glance with Dakota, neither of them commented on the absently spoken comment. He knew his mate hadn't meant anything by it. Helsinki had just been blurting out a thought.

Dane's softly spoken comment drew Dixon's attention. "I've sent a text to Delanrue," he murmured. "He'll set up a tracker to monitor Rian's movements. He said Mason is already under surveillance as of last week, but no report came through about anything out of the ordinary happening on Thursday night."

"Who's monitoring Mason?" Regales asked quietly.

Shrugging, Dane shook his head. "I'll ask for reports to be sent to you."

"I'll start looking into the pair's financials while you all are off running," Theo—Regales's human mate—told him. "Have him email me his deets as well as any known buddies." As Theo bent over and picked up a laptop bag Dixon hadn't even noticed—being near his unclaimed mate could definitely be distracting—he called, "Hey, Hels. Can you tell me any other names of your brother's buddies?"

"Why?" Helsinki turned his attention to the human. Cocking his head, he furrowed his eyebrows. "What are you doing?"

Theo lifted his focus from the laptop he was opening. "Well, it sounds like that fight club is illegal, so we need to help the human authorities shut it down." His smile appeared kind as he added, "It's the right thing to do." Then his expression shifted to one of sadness. "And if shifters are fighting humans, that's dangerous, and not just to the poor unwitting humans."

"What do you mean?" Helsinki asked quietly, his tone full of trepidation.

"I mean, if the police busts the operation, and Rian or one of his buddies is arrested and goes to jail, what happens when their wounds are tended and their blood is analyzed?"

Helsinki shrugged and shook his head, clearly not following.

Dixon squeezed Helsinki against him, gaining his attention. "It means if their blood is analyzed by a human doctor, it could endanger our ability to keep shifters a secret."

Gasping, Helsinki gaped at Dixon. "But that's like, the number one rule." He glanced around at everyone. "Never tell a human about shifters unless it's your mate."

Theo nodded. "Exactly. That's why I need to check into what's going on with Rian's friends." He grimaced, rubbing his hand over the top of his laptop. "We can't let any of them get caught by the police, so we have to stop them from going there anymore before we have the cops shut it down."

Helsinki nodded. "Okay." Then he rattled off a couple of names while Theo typed away on his laptop.

CHAPTER SIX

Shifting his weight from foot to foot, Helsinki felt his bear rumble excitedly in his mind. He peered about, admiring the forest around him with their leaves of varying shades of oranges and yellows. While the golf course had copses of trees, they were so manicured the fall colors hadn't started to hit them, yet.

"What do you think?" Dixon rested his hand on the small of Helsinki's back. "Is your bear ready to stretch his legs?"

Helsinki nodded. While a tremble of anticipation at the coming run thrummed through his body, another type of shiver worked through him, too. The way Dixon kept touching him in little ways—his back, his thigh, and his shoulders—set his blood on fire in ways he'd never before experienced.

"Yeah, I'm ready for a run," Helsinki admitted, his thoughts swirling around the feel of Dixon's touch. "Why do you keep touching me? Is that a normal couple thing?"

Having never been part of a couple, Helsinki hadn't given it much thought. After all, he'd never been interested in the women Rian or his friends had brought around. He certainly hadn't wanted to touch them much beyond getting his rocks off. Even that had been tough on occasion. Helsinki had sometimes had to imagine men to get his dick to harden for them—not that he would ever have admitted that to anyone.

Won't have to worry about that with Dixon. Wanna touch his skin so bad.

"Touching *is* a normal thing, especially for shifters," Dixon confirmed, sliding his arm around his waist. He settled his other on Helsinki's chest and rubbed over his torso. "You, however, seem a little touch-starved to me, so I plan to touch you a lot, until you get used to the feel of my hands on you."

Helsinki nodded, appreciating that Dixon had kept talking. From his final comment, he'd been able to figure out what touch-starved meant. He really liked the idea of the handsome blond touching him often.

"I like the way your fair skin looks so different compared to mine," Helsinki admitted, resting his own hand over Dixon's on his chest. "Are you naturally this fair?"

His own skin was quite a bit darker than Dixon's.

Dixon growled softly, which caused Helsinki's stomach to flip. Except, then Dixon turned his hand and threaded their fingers together, calming him. Leaning closer, Dixon even nuzzled his nose into Helsinki's neck.

"Yes, Hels," Dixon murmured against his skin, sending heat over his flesh and causing the hairs on his nape to stand on end. "If you like how our fingers look against each other, you'll love the look of our naked bodies pressed together." After speaking, Dixon nipped at Helsinki's neck, then stepped backward, a grin on his face. "Before I get carried away, let's strip and go on that run."

Helsinki bit back a groan. "If I get naked now, everyone's gonna see my hard sex," he grumbled, feeling his cheeks heat.

Dixon winked. "No, they won't." Turning, he pointed out the way the guys, who'd been joined by a couple of other big men, were standing quite a distance away. "They're giving us a measure of privacy." Waggling his brows, Dixon added huskily, "And I plan to get a very close and personal look at your cock . . . later."

Letting his groan out, Helsinki pressed the heel of his palm to his groin. "That was mean," he whined. "Now all I can think about is your face close to my crotch."

Laughing softly, Dixon whipped his shirt over his head. "Not mean. Just giving you something to anticipate," he countered. "Now hurry up, my mate."

Helsinki huffed a sigh even as he grabbed the hem of his t-shirt. After whipping it over his head, he folded it and placed it on his battered sneakers, which he'd toed off at the same time. He swiftly undid his fly and blew out in relief as the pressure eased on his erection.

With swift movements, Helsinki pushed his jeans off. He folded them, too, and placed them on his shirt. Finally, he removed his socks, folding one in on itself over the other and shoving them into his shoe under his shirt.

When Helsinki straightened, he did his best to ignore his jutting shaft. He cut a look Dixon's way from the corner of his eye and spotted the naked man openly staring at him. His cheeks heated, and he knew his face had to be bright red.

"Freckles are gonna stand out," Helsinki grumbled, rubbing over his face in discomfort. "Damn things."

"I happen to love your freckles, Helsinki," Dixon told him quietly. "But I don't wish to embarrass you. Do you want to meet the bears you don't know before we shift?"

Scowling at Dixon, Helsinki felt a measure of annoyance rise within him. "Couldn't we have met them before?" he grumbled. The response caused his prick to soften, though, so maybe that was a good thing.

Dixon grimaced. "Sorry, Hels." He shrugged, spreading his hands wide in placation. "You distracted me." Dipping his chin down, Dixon batted his eyelashes at him. "Forgive me?"

Helsinki's ire instantly evaporated to be replaced by mirth. "Stop that." Laughing, he reached out and shoved at Dixon's upper arm. "You look ridiculous."

Realizing what he'd said, he felt the blood drain from his face. Any residual trace of arousal died a quick death. He couldn't believe he'd just called a more dominant shifter ridiculous.

Fuck! What was I thinking?

"Whoa, whoa," Dixon called.

When Dixon wrapped his arms around him, Helsinki couldn't help but flinch.

"Please, relax, my mate," Dixon murmured into his ear, tightening his arms around him and flushing their chests together. "You're safe with me. Always." Nuzzling the side of his neck, Dixon licked along his tendon. "Yes, I'm dominant. That's true," he murmured into his ear. "Can't become a pack beta without that attribute, but you're my mate. You're my heart and soul, my everything. I'll *never* harm you."

Helsinki gave in to the happy rumble of his bear, which loved being in Dixon's arms. Whimpering ever-so-softly, he hunched his shoulders and pressed into Dixon's chest. The scent of Dixon's concern flooded Helsinki's nostrils, and for some reason, that settled him. Helsinki nestled his nose in the crook of Dixon's neck and enjoyed the comfort it caused.

"Sorry," Helsinki muttered, heaving out a deep breath.

"Don't apologize for your responses," Dixon chastised gently. "They help me learn about you, how to care for you, how to love you."

Lifting his head, Helsinki cocked his head. "Love me?" He didn't get it. "How can you love me already? We haven't even had sex."

Dixon smiled, the corners of his eyes crinkling a smidge. "No, I don't love you, just yet, but I know I'll fall very quickly if you let me." Waggling his brows, he added, "It's the nature of fated mates to lose their hearts to the other half of their soul." A second later, Dixon smirked. "And having sex with you will be beyond amazing, but that's not what will make us love each other."

"Really? Then what will?" Helsinki couldn't believe how different Dixon and Rian's beliefs were. "Rian says if sex isn't good, then she's not worth seeing twice. And he—"

Unwinding one arm lightning-fast, Dixon pressed his fore-fingers to Helsinki's lips, stalling his words. "Handsome, some of what your brother says"—he paused for a few seconds, a muscle ticking in his jaw—"well, his opinions leave me with a bad flavor in my mouth." Sliding his fingers off of Helsinki's lips, Dixon cradled his nape. "I just"—halting again, he squinted at Helsinki—"can't think of anything nice to say right now about his opinions."

Helsinki couldn't help but mumble, "My momma used to say, if you don't have anything nice to say, don't say nothin' at all."

Dixon chuckled. "Agreed." He winked. "So I'll keep my mouth shut."

Sighing, Helsinki decided to admit, "Rian don't do that. He doesn't care who he hurts with his words." Thinking on that, he shook his head. "Naw, more like the opposite."

"What do you mean?" Dixon asked.

With the way Dixon massaged his nape, Helsinki found his mind shutting down and his mouth answering honestly, without reservation. "Recently, I've noticed this gleam in Rian's eyes. It's sort of . . . malicious." He sighed, wondering when his brother had grown so mean. "He likes it when his words hurt." Swallowing hard, Helsinki finished, "Especially me." He realized what he said and blinked once, twice, trying to focus. "But why? I'm his brother. I clean the house and cook the food and do the laundry. Shouldn't he appreciate me?"

Helsinki watched Dixon blow out a breath through pursed lips. The way his blue eyes darkened to a stormy color coupled with the slightly acrid tinge to his scent told Helsinki the wolf shifter struggled with something. His desire to soothe came out of nowhere, but he went with it.

Wrapping his arms around Dixon in return, Helsinki gently placed his palms on the skin of the other shifter's back. He felt a zing of pleasure, enjoying the smooth flesh under his hands, even as he began rubbing up and down, just a little. Humming, Helsinki dipped his head the inch difference in their heights and nuzzled his cheek against Dixon's.

"I can give you an answer to your question, Hels," Dixon murmured, tipping his head and offering him more room.

And his neck. Holy shit! Why would Dixon, a more dominant shifter, offer that to me?

"Hels? You listening to me, my mate?"

Dixon's words drew Helsinki back to what they were talking about.

My brother.

"My brother would never have offered his neck to me," Helsinki mused absently. "He'd never offer his neck to anyone unless he absolutely had to. But you did. For me." He pulled his head back a little so he could look into Dixon's blue eyes. "Pretty eyes. They look like they should be ice-blue, but not when you look at me." Seeing the surprise fill Dixon's face, Helsinki grinned. "You're nothing like Rian."

A smile curved Dixon's full lips, and his eyes almost appeared to dance with pleasure—pleasure that Helsinki realized had nothing to do with sex.

Huh.

"Thank you for paying me the greatest of compliments, Helsinki," Dixon purred as he closed the distances between their faces.

Then Dixon touched his lips to Helsinki's, yanking a gasp from him. A tingle spread from where Dixon touched him, across his cheeks and down his neck. The hairs on his arms stood on end, and his hands began to tremble against Dixon's back.

Helsinki peered into Dixon's eyes, now the color of storm-gray, he saw the burning desire within their depths. He couldn't help the whine that escaped him, having never seen such a look directed at him. Feeling Dixon's tongue slide across his bottom lip, Helsinki barely managed to get enough air into his lungs.

"D-Dixon," Helsinki whimpered, a tremble working through him. "Wh-What?"

While the light touch of Dixon's lips didn't disappear altogether, it did lighten just a little. "Yes, my mate?" he murmured. "Is this okay?"

Okay?

"M-More than." Helsinki just couldn't seem to follow what was happening was all. Since Dixon had always seemed okay with his questions, he asked, "H-How did talking about my br-brother lead to this?"

To Helsinki's surprise, Dixon chuckled huskily. "Good question." After increasing the pressure on Helsinki's lips for a few more seconds in a chaste kiss that sent his pulse racing and his blood pounding, Dixon eased back. "Because you see that I'm different than your brother. That is a great gift from you." His expression turned sad. "Especially since, the answer to your earlier question, is that your brother says mean things to you, insults you, and hits you, because he wants to keep control over you. He wants you to think you have to do exactly as he says, because he doesn't want his slave labor, the person who cooks, cleans, and takes care of all the menial things he doesn't want to do, to go somewhere else."

Helsinki tried to follow all of Dixon's rambling words. He wasn't certain he completely followed, but he did understand one thing. "So, because I clean his house and stuff, he hits me and calls me names so I keep doing that?" Helsinki didn't get it. "Wouldn't he think that would make me want to leave?"

Dixon nodded once. "You would think so, but have you *ever* thought about leaving your brother?"

"No," Helsinki replied automatically. "Huh."

"Exactly." Dixon's smile appeared kind. "When people do that, it's a way of manipulating someone's mind into making the treatment seem normal." Sliding the fingers of his left hand up into Helsinki's hair, Dixon used a thumb to tuck a strand of hair behind his ear, creating a tingle to trickle down his neck. "A person will think there's no reason to look for something else, a better or different situation, because they think it's the same everywhere."

Helsinki processed that, and he scowled. "So I'm stupid."

Dixon growled as he tightened his hold in Helsinki's hair. Still, he didn't hurt him, just held his head steady so he couldn't look away.

"No, you are *not* stupid for this, Helsinki," Dixon declared. "The fault is with Rian. He chose to take advantage of your good and kind nature. He's an asshole for treating you that way." The storm-gray of arousal had long since disappeared, and an angry ice-blue remained. "Many people have fallen for the type of tricks he used on you. Those others aren't stupid, either, and neither are you." His expression eased, and he furrowed his brows. "Please tell me you understand the difference between believing someone's lies and being stupid."

Do I understand?

"But I'm a shifter," Helsinki pointed out slowly. "Shouldn't I have smelled when Rian lied to me?"

"Not if Rian believes what he's claiming," Dixon countered. "Even if what he's saying isn't an actual fact, if he believes it, his scent won't smell of lies."

A shiver worked down Helsinki's spine. "Th-Then he must believe a lot of lies."

Dixon nodded. "That is possible."

"Are you love-birds ready to run?" a deep voice asked from off to the left. "My bear wants to play."

Smiling, Dixon eased away from Helsinki. "Allow me to introduce Hess. He's a Kodiak bear shifter." Smirking, he rolled his eyes. "Fair warning, he loves to wrestle in bear form, but it's for fun, not to hurt."

Helsinki appreciated the subject change. He didn't want to

think about his brother anymore. Then Dixon's words regis-
tered, and he focused on the grinning, dark-haired man.

"You like to play? Really?"

Hess grinned back. "Yep."

"Okay!"

"Let's go then," Hess encouraged, then turned, obviously
comfortable in his nudity, and began to shift.

Dixon released Helsinki, and they both followed suit.

CHAPTER SEVEN

Dixon figured galloping through the forest with a bunch of bears probably shouldn't have been entertaining. Except, it was. Instead of constantly worrying whether or not the much larger predators intended to hand his wolf his ass, Dixon found himself chuffing every time Helsinki or Hess tackled each other.

The first time Dixon had seen Hess barrel into Helsinki's side, he'd almost pounced on the Kodiak's back with the intention of protecting his mate . . . with force. Fortunately, he'd stayed his instinct long enough to notice the happy gleam in Hess's bear's eyes. Hess had continued over the top of Helsinki's slightly larger polar bear, and they'd both tumbled sideways, rolling together.

With the way their limbs flailed and their jaws snapped at shoulders, Dixon realized that it was actually the bears playing. Even when Hess wrapped his jaws around Helsinki's upper foreleg and tugged, the scent of blood never perfumed the air. The Kodiak dragged the polar a few feet, then released him and bounced backward.

Helsinki lurched to his paws and returned the favor by lowering his head and lunging forward. Ramming his broad forehead into Hess's side, he forced Hess to stumble sideways. He followed that up by lumbering another step forward and lowering his head further. Then Helsinki jerked his head up and caused Hess to tumble and roll. His mate's polar bear pounced, grabbing Hess's foreleg and tugging.

After bounding after the pair for well over an hour, judging by the position of the sun, Dixon sat watching them lay on the forest floor, panting. Unable to help himself, he padded over to his bear. He sniffed at the male's forelegs, licking his fur.

Dixon's wolf made certain that, even though he didn't smell any blood, Helsinki wasn't injured. To his pleasure, his mate didn't have a scratch on him. For good measure, Dixon licked over the fur of his polar bear, removing Hess's scent.

Just as Dixon finished, Hess heaved to his feet and crossed to them. The Kodiak's tongue lolled from his mouth, and Dixon thought there was a definite look of mischief on the animal's face. Narrowing his eyes, Dixon growled low in his throat in warning.

Hess chuffed, mirth twinkling in the bear's brown eyes. Then the shifter focused on Helsinki and bumped his nose against the polar bear's foreleg. When Helsinki chuffed back and cocked his head curiously, Hess swung his head to the left.

Dixon watched Helsinki turn and follow the other bear's attention. Then he returned his gaze to Hess. When the Kodiak nudged Helsinki again before glancing left, Dixon peered in that direction.

While Dixon had noticed Kontra's bear head back toward the parking area almost ten minutes before in the company of a hyena who'd appeared and yipped for his attention, he spotted Dane in Komodo dragon form sprawled on a tree branch almost fifteen feet up. Underneath him and a little further away, Regales's grizzly sunned himself in a beam that filtered between trees. His eyes were closed, but occasionally, his ear twitched, telling Dixon that Regales wasn't really sleeping.

Still, with Regales's eyes closed, he obviously wasn't ready for what happened next.

Helsinki opened his mouth in a polar bear grin as he heaved to his paws. After he exchanged a glance with Hess, the pair broke into a gallop. They closed the distance between themselves and the councilman in seconds and pounced.

While Helsinki landed on Regales's haunch, Hess flopped over his shoulders.

Regales roared and surged upward. Well, he tried to, anyway. The other pair of bears easily kept him down and even rolled him to his back.

Dixon peered up at Dane, wondering how the enforcer would respond. To his relief, he saw the male manage an impressive feat of rolling his eyes. When Dane returned his focus to the trio, he appeared amused.

Creeping forward, Dixon sniffed the air. He knew Hess and Helsinki were playing, but he wasn't certain how forgiving Regales's bear would be. To his relief, there remained no scent of blood in the air even as the trio rolled around on the forest floor, growling and snapping.

Lying on his belly, Dixon waited for his mate and the other bears to have their fun. He watched in amusement, wondering when Helsinki had last had the opportunity to play like this. His mate had certainly seemed super excited by the opportunity, although Dixon had noticed the polar bear glancing his way a time or two while he did so.

My mate is keeping an eye on me.

While Dixon was more dominant, his wolf still appreciated that his bear cared about him. In fact, at one point, when Hess grew especially exuberant, rolling toward where Dixon watched, Helsinki had forced him to move in another direction. It didn't matter that Dixon could easily have trotted out of the way.

Finally, the trio of bears lay sprawled on the ground, panting heavily.

Regales was the first to shift. The councilman eased to a sitting position and scrubbed his hands through his salt and pepper hair. Chuckling as he peered at the other bears, he shook his head.

"How old are you, Hess? Fifteen?" Regales teased.

Hess's bear pursed his lips and did a fantastic job of blowing a raspberry.

Dane's Komodo dragon rumbled, the sound one of clear amusement.

Tipping his head back, Regales mock-scowled at the shifter enforcer. "And you? Where were you? You're supposed to have my back."

Shifting in seconds, Dane remained lying on the branch as he smirked at Regales. "As if you were in any real danger from those two."

"Yeah, yeah," Regales quipped back, although there was no real ire in his tone. "You just better hope your brother is doing a better job guarding my mate than you're doing for me."

Dane snorted. "You know as well as I do that Dakota would never let anything happen to Theo."

Dakota had moved from the front seat to the back of the limo to keep Theo company. Of course, considering the human had been engrossed in researching Rian's friends, Dakota wouldn't be getting much conversation from him. Seeing as Dixon had noticed Dakota pulling up a reading app on his phone before he'd started talking with Helsinki earlier, he figured the enforcer hadn't minded.

Regales's smile turned fond, making Dixon believe he was thinking of his mate. "Yeah. I'm glad Dakota and Theo hit it off so well," he stated, betraying his thoughts. "I'm ready to head back to him." Then Regales turned his attention to Dixon. "Dakota is telling Carson and Manon where to pick up you and Helsinki."

Confusion filling him, Dixon shifted. "Pick us up?" he asked as soon as he had the proper vocal cords. "What do you mean?"

"Ah, right." Regales glanced from Helsinki and back to Dixon. "I suppose I'm jumping the gun, and you haven't talked to him about that, yet."

"Talk to me about what?" Helsinki asked, having shifted right after Dixon had. He crawled over to Dixon, glancing between them nervously. "A-Am I in trouble for, um, pouncing on you, Councilman?" Settling on his butt beside Dixon, Helsinki drew his knees up to his chest and wrapped his arms around his shins. "I thought you were playin', too."

"You're not in trouble, Helsinki," Hess assured, having also shifted. "This isn't about our romping in bear form." The big male settled on his ass and lifted one knee, resting his forearms on it. Hess pointed at Dixon. "This is about you heading to Stone Ridge with your mate, since he lives there, and you'll finish your restitution there."

"I-I . . ." Helsinki glanced at Dixon, meeting his gaze for an instant with wide eyes, then peered back at Hess and Regales. "What?"

Regales chuckled softly, the sound full of kindness. "We kinda sprung that on you, didn't we?" Before Helsinki could respond, the councilman added, "Because you're Dixon's mate, who is a wolf shifter in a large pack with good standing to the council, you have the option of staying here and finishing your restitution, or you can leave with Dixon now and do some chores decided on between the council and Alpha Declan."

Helsinki's brows furrowed as he focused on Dixon. "Is that your alpha?"

Dixon nodded. "Alpha Declan McIntire." He suddenly realized he'd not spoken to his alpha personally since discovering Helsinki was his mate. Turning his attention to Regales, Dixon twisted his lips into a wry smile. "I assume you've spoken to Declan?"

Instead, Dane answered with a scoff. "Of course, we spoke with Alpha Declan before Regales said anything to Helsinki." The enforcer waggled his brows, and his expression appeared amused from where he was resting in the tree. "First, Declan laughed when he realized it was us calling about you meeting your mate and not you." Dane winked. "Then he offered his congratulations to you, and he asked us for more information about Helsinki."

Reaching over, Dixon gripped Helsinki's hand. "That sounds like him." He offered his mate a reassuring smile. "Alpha Declan welcomes all mates, whether they be human, vampire, shifter, or something else." Squeezing his mate's fingers, Dixon assured, "He's a good alpha, and those in Stone Ridge will welcome you."

"B-But—" Helsinki paused, nibbling his bottom lip.

Dixon guessed at what Helsinki was thinking—*what about my brother*—and tried to offer a compromise. "Well, I figure the council might order Rian to go through a rehabilitation course," he started, glancing up at Dane, who nodded his agreement. "But after that, we could arrange to have Rian moved to Stone Ridge, too. Well, if he's willing, anyway."

Helsinki's brows furrowed, and the spicy scent of confusion flooded Dixon's nostrils. "Huh?"

Realizing his assumption had been wrong, Dixon knew he needed clarification. "You started to say, but . . . something?" He squeezed Helsinki's hand. "I guessed you were going to ask about your brother, but that was obviously wrong. So . . . but *what*?"

Rubbing the back of his neck with his free hand, Helsinki mumbled, "But I worked for the rogue councilman." He glanced around, the spice of his nerves perfuming the air. "Why would he allow me in his territory? Aren't I considered the enemy?"

Dixon chuckled softly as he shook his head. "No, handsome." With a wink, he told his mate, "Alpha Declan and his pack have welcomed a few members who were once called enemies."

Nodding slowly, Helsinki didn't seem completely convinced.

I'll convince him, eventually.

"So, guess we should have asked," Dane commented from above. "Are you even open to moving?"

Dixon suddenly found it difficult to breathe. If his mate didn't want to move, he wasn't certain what he would do. He was just getting settled in his new pack with his new home, and he loved it there.

Could I uproot myself for my mate?

Fortunately, Dixon didn't have to come up with an answer to that.

"Oh, yeah. I can move," Helsinki stated. "What kind of restitution do you think I'll end up having to do there?" He appeared worried for a second before his lips curved into a hopeful smile. "Hey, I could muck stalls while you ride your horse. That don't take much brains, right?"

Biting back his desire to grimace — Dixon hated hearing Helsinki talking badly about himself — he forced a smile instead. "I'm sure Jerry would appreciate any help you want to give him, but I'd like to ride *with* you, too." He squeezed his mate's large hand. "And it's something we can discuss with Alpha Declan when we get there. Don't worry," he assured. "He'd never ask you to do anything degrading."

Helsinki nodded even as he worried his bottom lip.

"So," Dixon pressed, needing to hear the confirmation one more time. "Are you willing to run away with me?"

Grinning, Helsinki chuckled. "Yeah." He squeezed Dixon's hand. "I'll run away with you." His expression sobered as he turned serious. "I've never done anythin' just for myself before, and I'm feelin' like this is a little selfish, but I want it . . . more than I've ever wanted anything in my life."

Dixon leaned close, bumping his shoulder against Helsinki's. "Then we can be selfish together, my mate."

Helsinki's smile widened once more. "Okay."

"So, on that note," Hess cut in, waggling his brows. "We better be on our way." Then the bear began to shift.

Regales held up his hand, and Dixon paused before doing the same. "After you pack your room at council headquarters, Delanrue and Germaine will escort you and members of Dixon's pack to the home you've been sharing with Rian." A muscle ticked in his jaw as he explained, "They will oversee your time with your brother, just in case he has a number of friends with him when you go to gather whatever you have there and to say good-bye."

"I-I gotta go there?" Helsinki mumbled, not sounding as if he wanted to do that at all.

Dixon sort of agreed. He didn't want to see how Rian treated Helsinki. At least, not first hand.

"Would you prefer to make a list of what you want?" Dixon offered. "I can have one of my people go with the enforcers to get whatever you don't want to leave behind."

Helsinki sighed before shaking his head. "Naw. Councilman Regales is right. I should say good-bye to my brother." While rubbing the back of his neck, he added, "Don't know when I'll see him again, after all."

Dixon scented the uneasiness pouring off Helsinki in waves, but he couldn't tell if his mate was upset about not knowing when he would see his brother again or if it was the prospect of *having* to see him at all.

Regardless, I'll be by his side the entire time.

"Then we'll leave you to it," Regales stated. Then with a smirk and a wink, he added, "Feel free to take your time out here. I'm pretty sure it'll be at least twenty minutes before your pack-mates arrive."

Sucking in a sharp breath at the prospect of being alone with his mate for the first time, Dixon felt his half-hard prick swell. From the corner of his eye, he saw Helsinki shift as he glanced at Dixon, nibbling his bottom lip. The answering scent of his mate's arousal perfumed the air.

Dane chuckled as he dropped from the tree. "Sounds like they like that idea." After a wink, and ignoring Dixon's growl, the enforcer shifted.

Regales did the same, and both men headed through the trees, leaving them alone.

Dixon turned his attention to his mate. While Helsinki reeked of arousal, there was an underlying flavor of uncertainty, too.

With a smile, Dixon reached over and rested his hand on Helsinki's knee. "We'll go as slow as you need, my mate. There's no rush for anything."

To Dixon's surprise, Helsinki glanced toward where the other shifters had disappeared, then launched at him.

CHAPTER EIGHT

Helsinki knew Dixon thought he would be uncertain because he'd never done anything with a guy before. Nothing could have been further from what he wanted, though. His dick had never been so hard so often, and he wanted relief.

Plus, Dixon's smell was driving him crazy.

Wrapping his arms around Dixon's shoulders, Helsinki took them both to the ground. He sprawled over the muscular man, peering down at him. His flesh almost felt as if it burned everywhere the other shifter's naked skin slid against his own.

"Oh, gods," Helsinki moaned, rubbing his hard sex against Dixon's thigh. "Feels so good!"

Dixon's arms wrapped around his torso, rubbing over his back. "Damn straight, it does," he rumbled. Tightening his hold on Helsinki's hips, Dixon encouraged his rutting while bucking his own hips.

Feeling Dixon's thick erection pressed against his side, Helsinki paused. He tensed for a second before burying his face in Dixon's neck. Inhaling deeply of the wolf shifter's delicious aroma, Helsinki began to rut once more.

"Take what you need, my mate," Dixon encouraged, gliding his hands up his back, then down again. Not stopping at Helsinki's hips that time, Dixon gripped his ass cheeks and squeezed, massaging his globes. "I want you to spill your seed, Hels," Dixon purred into his ear. "Coat me with your scent. Make me smell like you."

Helsinki's bear rumbled possessively in his mind, and he agreed wholeheartedly with his animal. He wanted to do exactly that. Everyone would know that he'd lain in Dixon's arms.

"Yesss," Helsinki growled. "Gonna pour my spunk all over you." Lifting a little, he peered between them. At the same time, Helsinki eased sideways so he straddled Dixon's thighs. "Gonna mark you inside and out."

Dixon moaned and bucked up against him. "Hell, yeah."

Hearing Dixon's acceptance somehow managed to ramp up Helsinki's arousal. His cock throbbed and twitched where it was pressed against his new lover's. Pre-cum drooled from his crown, dripping onto the other man's sex.

Helsinki couldn't ever remember seeing anything so spine-tingling.

"I'm dripping on you, Dix," Helsinki muttered. "Fuck, that's sexy."

Peeling a hand off Dixon's shoulder, Helsinki reached between them. He hesitated just an instant before swiping his fingertips over where he'd drooled on Dixon's erection. Excitement and need surged through him upon his first touch of another guy's dick.

And this is my mate!

Dixon hummed, causing Helsinki to glance at his face. Seeing a smile curving his lips as the other shifter watched him feeling up his erection, he grinned and returned his focus to Dixon's cock. Doing his best to ignore his aching prick, Helsinki fondled his lover's length, touching and exploring.

"Wow," Helsinki mumbled. "You feel so similar to me, but different, too." Sliding his fingertip over Dixon's cock head, he scooped up a large bead of pre-cum. Helsinki lifted his focus to Dixon's face when he heard the wolf shifter's soft growl. Seeing the feral glow of desire burning in Dixon's blue-eyed gaze, Helsinki grinned and slipped his finger into his mouth. When the bit of fluid teased his taste buds with

Dixon's mild flavor, Helsinki hummed. "Pre-cum tastes similar to mine. Wonder if your seed will, too."

"Turn around so we can suck each other, and you can find out," Dixon stated gruffly, his hands flexing and relaxing on Helsinki's ass.

With his mind swimming with arousal, Helsinki took a second to process Dixon's growled comment. "Really? You'd suck my cock?" He lifted his brows and cocked his head. "But you're obviously the more dominant of us. Why would you do that?"

Helsinki hadn't considered that possibility.

"Oh, Hels," Dixon crooned, lifting a hand to cradle his jaw. "I would never expect you to do something I wouldn't."

"Really?"

Dixon grinned, nodding once. "We're partners, my mate," he told him, teasing his thumb along his lower lip. "While I have every intention of claiming your ass as soon as we have the necessary supplies, I'm more than willing to bottom for you, too."

Gaping, Helsinki felt a shudder work through him. His cock twitched just at the idea of sinking into Dixon's gorgeous globes. Before shifting, he'd had a hell of a time stopping himself from staring at Dixon's tight ass.

Chuckling, Dixon used a couple of crooked fingertips to encourage Helsinki's mouth closed. Then he slid his fingers around to grip his nape. Dixon exerted a bit of pressure, urging him closer.

"Come down here and kiss me, Helsinki," Dixon encouraged. "Grip us both or just rut to completion. My balls need to bathe your belly in my seed so fucking badly." After a wink, he added, "Then we can lick it off each other before turning around and mouthing each other's cocks. I wanna drown in your scent, my mate."

Helsinki groaned as his sex twitched upon hearing Dixon's

words. "Yes." Then he obeyed.

Lowering his head, Helsinki pressed his lips to Dixon's. He had a little experience with kissing women but never a man, and he wasn't certain what to expect. To his surprise, Dixon's lips felt soft against his own, moving gently as he coaxed him to open.

Goose bumps broke out on his neck and shoulders as Helsinki parted his lips. He welcomed Dixon's tongue into his mouth. While he expected the other man to plunder him, Dixon didn't. Instead, he teased along his tongue, encouraging Helsinki into tongue-play he'd never before experienced.

Dixon threaded his hand into Helsinki's hair and used the hold to tilt his head a bit. His tongue pushed deeper, mapping him slowly. At the same time, Dixon banded his other arm around his ass and began rocking.

Moaning at the multiple points of stimulation, Helsinki felt his boiling blood course through his veins. He shuddered in Dixon's hold and began rutting, too. His cock throbbed, and his nipples beaded. His skin felt too hot, yet not hot enough where he was pressed flush to Dixon from chest to thighs.

Helsinki's mind swam, his pleasure causing his senses to reel. Even sinking his dick into a woman hadn't caused his blood to burn in such a way. He couldn't seem to get close enough to Dixon, and he groaned into the other man's mouth.

Breaking the kiss, Dixon pressed Helsinki's face against the crook of his neck. "Come for me, Helsinki," he whispered into his ear. "Bathe me in your seed. Coat my belly. Warm my skin."

Whimpering, Helsinki felt his balls tighten. He pressed harder against the other man's groin, reveling in the feel of the hard length sliding against his own. His desire to obey surged through him, and his body flushed hot, his orgasm barreling through his veins.

Shaking and shuddering in Dixon's hold, Helsinki moaned

as heady bliss coursed through his system. Fire zipped along his veins, heating him from the inside out. As the scent of his cum filled the air, Helsinki noted another aroma, too — Dixon's seed.

Helsinki groaned at the wonderful smell, his mouth watering. His canines lengthened. Sucking in a harsh breath at the odd sensation, he took in a deep lungful of Dixon's scent.

Before Helsinki realized what he was doing, he wrapped his jaw around Dixon's flesh . . . and bit. When the iron-rich fluid poured across his tongue, he jolted at the exquisite taste. He swallowed before deepening his teeth and sucking hard, wanting more, so much more.

Dixon shuddered beneath him, catching Helsinki's attention. He gasped in shock at his actions, pulling his teeth free. Seeing the deep punctures caused by his canines and the blood pooling from the twin wounds to drip down Dixon's neck, Helsinki winced.

"Oh, shit," Helsinki whispered. "I'm so sorry."

"I'm not," Dixon countered, yanking Helsinki's attention to his lover's face. A sated smile curved his lips, and he winked — actually *winked*! "I would appreciate it if you'd close the wounds, though." Glancing at his shoulder, Dixon urged, "You mind?"

For a second, Helsinki wasn't certain what Dixon meant. Then he realized what the man must be asking for. Dipping his head, he quickly swiped his tongue over the puncture wounds, sealing them. In the process, Helsinki received another round of enjoying Dixon's delicious flavor.

Helsinki moaned and licked again, unable to help himself. He quickly cleared away all the blood. To his shock, he felt his bear rumble contentedly in his mind even as the desire to bite Dixon again surged through him.

Mortified, Helsinki flung himself off Dixon. He scrambled back a couple of feet as he stared at his lover. Uncertainty and fear sizzled through his veins, removing any last traces of the afterglow from the best damn orgasm of his life.

"Hey. Hey," Dixon murmured, sitting up. His brows furrowed, and he sported a look of concern that Helsinki didn't understand. "Hels? What's wrong?" Lifting his hand, palm up, Dixon rumbled, "Take a couple of deep breaths, my mate. I understand that your first time with a guy can be . . . different, but please don't freak out on me." Wiggling his fingers, he urged, "Come back. Tell me what's going through that head of yours."

Freezing, Helsinki stared at Dixon as if he had two heads. "You think I'm freaking out because you're a guy?" He couldn't help it. He scoffed as he shook his head. "No, that was amazing. Awesome. Out of this world beyond anything I could ever have imagined."

Dixon's brows furrowed, and he tipped his chin down as he stared at him in obvious confusion. "Then what's the matter, Hels?"

How could he ask that?

"I bit you," Helsinki blurted out.

To Helsinki's shock, Dixon grinned . . . broadly. "And gods it was just as epic as other mated shifters have told me." His chuckle sounded husky. "I can't wait for you to do it again."

"What?" Helsinki gaped, beyond confused. "Y-You want me . . . again?" He shook his head. "B-But . . . why?"

Bending one leg and planting that foot on the ground, Dixon settled his outstretched arm on his knee. "I'm a bit confused as to why you would think I *wouldn't* want my mate to claim me, Hels," Dixon told him, still beckoning with his fingers.

"But you're the more dominant shifter," Helsinki pointed out even as he reached out and slid his hand into Dixon's. "You're supposed to bite me." Feeling Dixon's fingers squeeze him, Helsinki whispered, "Aren't you?"

Dixon lowered his leg and tugged lightly, urging Helsinki

to return to him. "There is no rule about that," he claimed even as his brows furrowed. "Let me guess. Rian told you that?"

Helsinki nodded as he knee-walked back to Dixon.

Wrapping his other arm around Helsinki, Dixon relaxed backward again, drawing Helsinki with him. "Who claims who is a personal decision between couples," Dixon told him, tucking him close to his side. "And if you'd asked before biting me, I would have said, *hell, yes, bite me, handsome.*" Sharing those last words, Dixon waggled his eyebrows as he grinned broadly at him.

Relaxing in Dixon's arms, Helsinki sighed deeply. "I probably should have asked first, huh?"

"If I'd been human, absolutely," Dixon replied, clearly being honest. "But I'm a shifter, too, so I expected it eventually."

"Huh." Helsinki nodded absently. "Did you really mean it when you said that you'd want me to bite you again?" Just thinking of Dixon's blood's delicious flavor caused his mouth to water once more.

Dixon chuckled. "Oh, hell, yeah, Hels." Cradling Helsinki's jaw, Dixon urged him to meet his gaze. "You didn't realize your bite made me come, did you?"

"It did?" Helsinki gaped for a second before admitting, "I thought you shuddered from pain."

Shaking his head, Dixon continued to grin. "Nope." He winked while curving his lips into a lascivious smile. "And I'm damn certain you'll come when I bite and claim you." Lifting a hand, Dixon traced his fingertip along Helsinki's tendon. "Right about here."

A shiver worked down Helsinki's spine, causing a warm flush to erupt over his skin. "Oh, wow." Giving Dixon a hopeful smile, he asked, "Now?"

"Your wish is my command, my mate," Dixon replied as he urged him onto his back. His expression grew more serious as he peered down at him. "Although our bond won't be entirely complete until one of us spills in the other."

Helsinki nodded, and he clenched his chute. To his surprise, he felt anticipation instead of dread. While he might be the bigger guy and his animal was a bear, Helsinki couldn't wait to submit to his wolf.

"Now?" Helsinki asked hopefully.

Dixon shook his head. "No supplies, remember?"

"Supplies?"

"Lube, Hels," Dixon told him. "I refuse to take your virgin ass without plenty of prep to make you comfortable." Skimming the backs of his forefingers along Helsinki's jaw, Dixon explained, "I never want to hurt you. Never."

Helsinki's heart thudded in his chest as he stared into Dixon's pale blue eyes. He felt the hairs on his arms stand on end. The sincerity in Dixon's eyes and filling his tone even caused his belly to flutter.

"Wow."

Dixon grinned, obviously liking his response. "Now, how about I show you just how great a claiming bite feels, and why I want you to bite me anytime you get the urge." Then he winked. "Well, unless we're in a room full of people. That could get awkward."

Chuckling, Helsinki nodded. "Okay."

"Now then." Dixon gripped Helsinki's hair and urged him to tip his head to the side, baring his throat to his wolf. "Lie back and enjoy."

Helsinki felt a momentary flash of fear when he watched Dixon's canines grow. His mate petting his throat and whispering words of encouragement calmed him. When Dixon started sucking on Helsinki's neck, his blood heated and began to fill his cock.

Then Dixon sank his teeth into Helsinki's neck, and he gasped at the flash of pain. Before he could even open his mouth to cry out, a wash of tingling heat flowed outward from the bite. His nipples beaded, his gut clenched, and his balls pulled tight.

Moaning roughly, Helsinki gave in to the heady wash of endorphins as Dixon sucked on his neck and a fresh orgasm crashed through his system.

CHAPTER NINE

Dixon reached over and squeezed Helsinki's hand as he watched his mate nibble his bottom lip. His lover stared out the SUV window at the house they were parked in front of. Hating the stench of uncertainty filling the cab, Dixon searched for a way to dispel it.

"You know you don't have to go in if you don't want," Dixon reminded him. He spotted another vehicle pull up behind his pack's own and recognized it as being from the Shifter Council. "The council enforcers just pulled up" — they'd reached Helsinki's home first and had been sitting in their vehicle for the last five minutes — "so it's not too late to just make a list."

Helsinki sighed deeply before turning his attention to Dixon. "I need to say good-bye, even though I'm sure I'm gonna get an earful." He reached up and touched Dixon's claiming bite, the edge of the mark just visible above the neckline of his t-shirt. "He won't approve of this."

"Perhaps after taking the shifter education course Enforcer Delanrue is going to tell Rian he must partake in, he'll eventually be happy for you." Dixon didn't really believe it, but his instinct drove him to offer his mate the chance at some hope that he wasn't losing his only family. Squeezing Helsinki's fingers, Dixon reminded, "Finding a fated mate is a gift, and he should be happy for you." He forced a soft chuckle. "And maybe even be a little jealous that you found yours first."

Helsinki's smile held a wealth of sadness. "I'm glad the enforcers are here," he stated, pointing across the street. "That's Mason's car, and Tanner is here, too. That's his truck in the driveway. Rian's would be in the garage."

"Do you have a vehicle?" Dixon asked curiously. "It's a long drive to Stone Ridge, but we could have it shipped."

Shaking his head, Helsinki grabbed the door handle and opened the door. "Naw, Rian says I'm not responsible enough to handle maintenance on it. I walked to work or took the bus."

Scoffing, Dixon followed Helsinki out of the SUV. "So, you're not responsible enough to take care of a car, but he expects you to handle the cooking and cleaning of the house, as well as using the bus system to get to work on time." Seeing Helsinki's shoulders hunch, Dixon realized he should have held his tongue. He gripped Helsinki's wrist and tugged, urging him to face him. "I shouldn't have spoken in such a derogatory way about your brother. My apologies."

Helsinki cocked his head. "A derogatory way?"

Dixon cleared his throat, trying to think of a way to clarify. "Uh, an expression for saying something unflattering about someone or something."

"Oh." Helsinki rubbed the back of his neck. "You use a lot of odd phrases. Is it common out where you are?"

Sliding his hand down from Helsinki's wrist so he could thread their fingers together, Dixon shrugged. "To be honest, I became pack beta just a few years ago. Before that, I lived in a small town in Minnesota." With a wink, Dixon told him, "Maybe the expressions are from there."

Helsinki nodded, smiling. "Okay." Then his apparent happiness faded. "Do you care that I ask when I don't understand?"

Squeezing Helsinki's fingers, Dixon admitted, "I love that you trust me enough to ask."

"Why?"

"Because I feel honored by your faith in me." Dixon could still see the confusion in Helsinki's expressive hazel eyes. "It means you're willing to admit your ignorance, knowing I won't think less of you that you need something explained."

Sighing in obvious relief, Helsinki grinned. "Okay."

The front door banging open broke into their moment. "Helsinki," a man called, drawing Dixon's attention. "What are you doing here with enforcers?" He crossed his arms over his chest. "Did you fuck up, brother?"

So this asshat is Rian. Great.

Even across the front yard, Dixon felt the dominance of the bear shifter standing on the porch. While similar to Helsinki in height and weight—standing six-foot-four with broad shoulders and a heavily built frame—that was where the similarities ended. Instead of warm hazel eyes, Rian's were a dark brown holding a cruel gleam. While Helsinki had an adorable pooch and love handles, Rian's trim waist showed he must work out . . . a lot . . . to counter the natural tendency for a polar bear to have a little extra around the middle, even in human form.

"No, I didn't mess up," Helsinki stated. While his voice was soft, Dixon knew it would carry to the other shifter. "I found my mate."

Rian narrowed his eyes as he swept his gaze over the group. "Oh, yeah? So where is she?"

Dixon and Helsinki had been joined by his pack-mates Manon, Carson, and Jared. Enforcers Delanrue and Germaine were striding from their SUV and already headed up the walk. There wasn't a woman in sight.

"No, woman," Jared cut in, taking the lead and following the council enforcers up the walk. He sported a wide smile and appeared so very pleased. "Your brother has been blessed to find his mate in our pack beta. Quite the catch, or so I've been told."

Seeing the mischievous gleam in Jared's hazel eyes, Dixon cast a pointed look at Carson. The head enforcer's lips twitched just a little as he shrugged before following his mate. Manon snickered, then headed after them.

Dixon understood as he started after them. Carson's mate had a bit of a mouth on him and loved stirring the pot, as the saying went. He'd also overheard stories about how, for a number of couples, he'd acted as the pack yenta. Then there were the tales of his blood-thirsty nature, and Dixon knew the human had made his living as an assassin for over a decade before mating with Carson and settling down — sort of.

Rian snarled, his lips curling away from his teeth. Pinning an angry sneer on Helsinki, he barked, "Helsinki, tell me you didn't go against everything you've ever been taught." He rested his hands on the porch railing and squeezed so hard Dixon heard the wood beneath his beefy mitts creak. "Assure me you haven't brought shame to our family name."

To Dixon's pride, Helsinki straightened where he walked beside him. "I didn't bring shame to our family," he claimed, although his voice came out soft. "I found my fated mate. That means I've been blessed."

"How many times do I have to tell your dumb ass that — " Rian snapped his mouth shut, taking a step back when Enforcer Delanrue and Enforcer Germaine took the four steps in one stride. Focusing on them, Rian asked, "What can I help you with today, Enforcers?"

While Rian dipped his head just a smidge in deference to their station, his tone was anything but respectful.

"We're here to supervise Helsinki packing his belongings," Enforcer Delanrue stated while crossing his arms over his chest. "I understand you have been keeping his checking, savings, and investment information for him as well as the contract he signed with the council. Please get that information now."

Rian looked like he wanted to refuse. His cheeks flushed. He opened and closed his mouth once, twice, before pinning an angry glare on Helsinki. Finally, Rian jerked a nod.

"He doesn't have any savings or investments," Rian stated. "But I do keep his checkbook and debit card. Otherwise, he'd always be in the red."

Dixon scowled. "That's not what Helsinki told us," he stated, climbing the stairs to the porch. "He says you take fifty percent of each paycheck. Thirty percent for lodging and utilities, ten percent to a savings account, and the final ten percent into some kind of investment."

Without bothering to spare Dixon a glance, Rian turned toward the front door. "I'll get his checkbook and debit card." As he moved through the open door, he claimed, "I had him leave both here since he wouldn't need any money while staying at council headquarters."

"Rian," Enforcer Germaine rumbled, stalking after him. "What happened to the twenty percent of Helsinki's checks that should have gone into savings and investments?"

Glancing over his shoulder, Rian shrugged. "I don't know what to tell you," he stated flippantly. "He lied to you."

"Or you're lying to us," Carson stated on a growl. "It's all over your scent."

Rian spun and began advancing on Carson. "Who the fuck do you think you are comin' into my home and callin' me a liar?" Lifting a hand, his intention to poke Carson in the chest clear as day, Rian kept talking. "Get out. No one invited you in here."

"I'm Carson Angeni, and I'm head enforcer for the Stone Ridge wolf pack." Carson kept his hands loose at his sides, obviously ready, even as he narrowed his eyes and sized Rian up. "This is Enforcer Manon as well as my mate, Jared. We're here in support of Beta Dixon and his mate, Helsinki."

Jared snickered. "Yeah. Just in case they need extra hands

carrying Helsinki's stuff out."

"His stuff?" Rian made a grab for Carson's arm, but Delanrue gripped his wrist, stopping him. While narrowing his eyes in obvious anger, Rian pulled back. "What the hell are you talking about?"

Sighing dramatically, Jared turned his attention to Helsinki. "Damn, Hels. You didn't tell us your brother was hard of hearing." Raising his voice, Jared stated in loud, well-enunciated words, "Like Enforcer Delanrue told you. We are here to get Hels's stuff so he can move in with his mate." Jared lifted a hand, palm up, and indicated Dixon. "This is Dixon Holsteen, beta of the Stone Ridge wolf pack. Hels is moving to Colorado to live with him."

The more Jared spoke, the darker red Rian's face became. Roaring, he lunged forward. Once again, Delanrue went to intercede. Jared didn't give him a chance.

Stepping forward and to the right, Jared grabbed Rian's arm. He used the shifter's momentum to swing him . . . right into Delanrue's arms.

Delanrue grunted, but recovered swiftly, catching Rian's upper arms, steadying them both.

"You saw that, Enforcers," Rian roared, yanking away to point at Jared. "That human fag attacked me in my own home. I want him brought before the council." Curling his lip, Rian continued to rant, "I warned my friends that trying to mate with humans would be shifters' downfall. They have no respect for our kind or our ways. They—"

"Stuff a cork in it, Rian," Germaine grumbled, scowling. "All I saw was a human avoiding getting attacked by an asshole."

Sucking in a harsh breath, Rian glared at Germaine. "Of course you'd side with him," he snarled. "Get the fuck out of my house."

"As soon as Helsinki gets all his belongings," Delanrue

countered, grabbing the back of Rian's neck. "Now, where are his financial papers, and don't give me any shit about his savings and investments. We all scented your lies."

"Hey, Rian," Mason appeared at the entrance to the foyer where the action had been happening. "Everything okay, man?"

Another man—a black-haired male with beady blue eyes—stood behind Mason, taking in the scene.

"That's Tanner," Helsinki mumbled helpfully.

Attempting to pull free of Delanrue, Rian jerked to the left. It didn't work. With a glare fixed on his features, he answered Mason's question.

"My dumb fuck brother finally gave into his fag urges," Rian declared. "Now he's leaving, which is good." He sneered at Helsinki. "Because he'll never be welcomed in my house again."

Dixon wanted to deck Rian as he took in the sadness permeating Helsinki's scent. "Hels, let's get your stuff," he encouraged, releasing his hand so he could place his hand on the small of his back. "Show me to your room, hmm?"

Helsinki nodded, and Delanrue pushed Rian out of their way. "I'll have Rian show me where he keeps financial information and see what I can find," he told everyone. Turning his attention to Germaine, he ordered, "See that these two stay in the living room and out of the way."

Germaine nodded, then headed toward Mason and Tanner, who immediately backed away from the slender anaconda shifter enforcer.

When Dixon crossed the threshold, he decided getting in and out as fast as possible was definitely a good idea—and not because Rian obviously didn't want them there. The place stank of beer, body odor, and spoiled food. He didn't even want to see the state of the kitchen or bathroom, especially after recalling how Rian had told Helsinki that he wanted him home soon to clean.

"Gods," Dixon muttered. "Your brother is" — he just stopped himself from saying *a pig*. Instead, he gritted his teeth and finished — "housework challenged."

Helsinki heaved a huge sigh as he peered around the place. "I don't envy whoever Rian gets to clean," he mumbled. "This place is a disaster."

Dixon nodded. "So, where's your room, handsome?"

Leading the way, Helsinki followed Rian and Delanrue down the hall. While the pair continued to the end of the hallway, his mate stopped at an open door on the left. When they stepped inside, Helsinki gasped before letting out a whimper.

"Well, fuck me," Manon muttered from behind them. "What the hell happened?"

"Someone was looking for something," Jared offered the idea. "Because this place is tossed."

Dixon silently agreed with Jared. The room was in a state of chaos. The dresser drawers, nightstand, and closet doors were all open. Clothes were piled on an unmade bed, the sheets having been pulled from the corners. A huge amount of paperbacks had been tossed on the floor, emptying the bookshelf.

Helsinki inhaled slowly, drawing Dixon's attention. As he panned his gaze around the room, a sheen filled his eyes. Shaking his head, he started toward the almost empty bookshelf.

"Someone was looking for this," Helsinki muttered, pushing the bookshelf to the left and out a foot. Then he pried off the baseboard behind it, revealing a hole. From within, Helsinki pulled a fabric bundle. Unwrapping it, Helsinki revealed a gorgeous brooch — a deep red gem dominated the middle with thin gold filaments making up the setting and holding a number of green stones in a pretty arrangement around it. "It belonged to my mother," Helsinki stated. "The only thing I have left of her. Everything else went to Rian, but she knew how much I loved this one piece, so she left it to me in her will." With a shrug, he added, "I don't know what happened to any of her other jewelry."

"It *all* should have come to me. *I'm* the older brother," Rian stated from the doorway. With hate-filled eyes, he flicked his gaze to the hole in the baseboard and back to Helsinki. "So that's where you hid it. I'll get it from you eventually." Rian scoffed as he tossed a folder onto the messy bed. "There's your checking account shit."

Then Rian turned and exited, Delanrue allowing him to pass. The dragon shifter sighed deeply as he shook his head. "I'm sorry, Hels," the enforcer stated softly. "Rian never opened a savings or investment account for you. I'm not certain what he spent that money on. If you want to put together a financial brief and submit it to the council, I'll make certain they force him to start paying you back."

Helsinki picked up the folder and flipped it open. A recent bank statement was right on top, showing a balance of a little over three hundred dollars. Sighing deeply, Helsinki shook his head.

"I'll think about it," Helsinki mumbled as he closed the file and turned to meet Dixon's gaze. "Can we just get some stuff together and leave?"

Dixon would do damn near anything to remove the sadness filling Helsinki's eyes. "Absolutely, my mate. Let's get everything wrapped up."

Then he and his pack-members started gathering his mate's things.

CHAPTER TEN

Helsinki walked down the barn aisle with a pitchfork in one hand while pulling a muck bucket behind him. His shoulders hurt a little from cleaning a dozen stalls — one of the volunteers had called in sick — but he still looked forward to his riding lesson. He couldn't believe how much fun riding a horse was.

As a bear shifter, getting on the back of a horse had never crossed Helsinki's mind. He was just over sixty years old, so cars were a regular thing ever since he was little. His small clan of bears had kept goats for milk and meat, but no one had ever had a horse.

Then, when Helsinki's mother had passed, Rian had decided to leave the clan. He'd convinced Helsinki to go with him. Being his only family, he'd thought his brother wanted him at his side due to that.

Now I know better.

Pushing memories of Rian and his . . . abuse . . . out of his mind, Helsinki headed toward the storage room so he could put away his supplies.

Gods, I hate thinking that, but Dixon explained it to me. Plus, he got me into therapy.

There was an elephant shifter in the Stone Ridge pack that was a psychiatrist — Gordon Digby. He was helping Helsinki come to understand Rian's actions. Well, at least, Gordon was helping him put his brother's abuse behind him.

"Hels?"

Upon hearing Dixon's call, Helsinki grinned. "In the storage room," he replied. "Be right there."

Helsinki settled the rake in its place against the wall, then pushed the muck bucket in its metal rolling frame where it should go. By the time he turned around, Dixon was lounging against the door frame. Taking in the muscular wolf shifter's breeches and polo-shirt-clad frame, Helsinki couldn't help humming in appreciation.

That was something else Helsinki was learning to accept — that it was okay for him to ogle his male mate.

It helped that half the pack were in homosexual matings.

"Hi, handsome," Dixon greeted, a hungry smile twisting his lips. "See something you like?"

Helsinki nodded, heading toward his wolf shifter. Resting his hands on Dixon's waist, he tugged the man forward. "And I know just what to do about it." Then Helsinki dipped his head and pressed his lips to Dixon's.

Just like every time they kissed, which was often, Dixon allowed Helsinki to lead for a few seconds. Then he quickly took over. Helsinki privately reveled in it when he did. He loved submitting to his dominant wolf.

After several minutes making out with Dixon, Helsinki heard the laughter of children. His mate immediately brought the kiss to an end, groaning softly under his breath. Dixon frowned at Helsinki, but there was still a twinkle in his pale blue eyes.

"You do make me forget myself," Dixon murmured, smiling warmly at him. Then he sobered and glanced down with a growl. "But riding with a boner is not comfortable, and it's clearly visible in these damn breeches, so I'm gonna have to step away for a few minutes to get it under control."

Helsinki glanced behind him, seeing no one near. "I have a better idea." Grabbing Dixon's hand, he hustled them out of the storage room and around the corner to the bathroom.

"Come on."

Dixon followed, a low chuckle rumbling from him. "What's on your mind, mate?"

Once in the bathroom, Helsinki closed and locked the door. He made quick work of Dixon's belt, then his own. After pulling a single-use package of lube from his jeans pocket, Helsinki pushed them down to his thighs.

Groaning softly, Dixon muttered, "Oh, fuck, Hels. I do like the way you think."

In the next instant, Helsinki allowed Dixon to spin him around to face the locked door. His mate took the packet of lube, so Helsinki placed his forearms on the wood. Then he arched his back and stuck out his ass.

"Hels," Dixon whispered roughly, clearly trying to keep it down. Rubbing his fingertips along the center of Helsinki's crack, he teased his opening. "Never get enough of you."

"Good. Been too long," Helsinki claimed. In truth, it had only been about six hours since they'd risen from their bed after a morning round. Except, Helsinki couldn't seem to get enough of Dixon's cock up his ass. "Please, take me."

"Yessss," Dixon hissed.

Helsinki sighed with satisfaction when he felt the semi-warmed slick—from being in his pocket for hours—against his anus. When Dixon pushed two fingers into his rectum and teased over his prostate, he bit his lip to keep from crying out his pleasure. Reaching left, Helsinki twisted the knob for the fan, hoping it would dampen the scent of their pheromones to whichever adult entered the room next.

Dixon chuckled huskily as he eased his fingers out. "I don't think we'll be in here long enough for our scents to build up too much," he purred into Helsinki's ear as he pressed his cock head against Helsinki's opening. "I'm gonna take you hard and fast, my mate, and you're gonna catch your spend in your hand so we can drink it together."

Biting his lip, Helsinki fought to keep in his moans. He loved sharing their seed—whether Dixon's or his own didn't matter. It made blowjobs and frotting just as pleasurable as fucking, since they could enjoy a treat in post-coital bliss afterward.

"Knock, knock," Dixon teased, tapping his cock against his hole. Then he pushed in. "Here I come."

"Yessss," Helsinki hissed, pushing back into his lover. Feeling his muscles stretch to accept his mate's thick girth, he couldn't help groaning under his breath. "So good."

"Oh, Hels." Dixon rested against his back, his arms tight around his waist. Licking along his neck, he purred, "You're so fucking perfect."

Helsinki knew that wasn't true, but with his mind clouded with the pleasure of Dixon's dick rubbing against his prostate, he couldn't form the words necessary to counter him. Instead, he whined and trembled in his lover's hold. He clenched and released his chute muscles, relishing the feel of Dixon's erection buried inside his body.

Nothing had ever been so perfect as coupling with his mate.

"My mate," Helsinki mumbled, loving how that sounded. "All mine."

With the way Dixon growled behind him, Helsinki knew his wolf enjoyed hearing it just as much.

"That's right, Helsinki," Dixon purred into his ear as he started to move. "You're mine, and I'm yours." He nipped at Helsinki's ear, sending sparks down his neck. "Love marking you, spilling in you, making you smell like me."

With one forearm on the door, Helsinki gripped his dick with his other. "Yes, please," he whined, wanting to smell like his wolf so badly. Something about their combined scents pleased his bear in a way nothing else ever had. "Love smelling like you. Like yours," he amended.

"Hell, yeah," Dixon muttered, his rutting picking up speed. "Been waiting so damn long for you. Love having you in my arms, in my home, in my life."

Helsinki groaned softly upon listening to Dixon's words. He'd learned that his mate mumbled the damnedest things while fucking, and he loved hearing them. His mate's assurances of how they belonged together were a balm to his battered soul.

It helped that Dixon followed up his mutterings with action, never raising a hand or comment against him. While Helsinki wasn't certain he believed all of his mate's compliments, he loved hearing them anyway. Dixon's loving words and actions made Helsinki's heart sing.

Unable to help himself, Helsinki blurted, "I love you."

Dixon froze behind him.

Realizing what he'd said, he cringed, tension ratcheting through his body. He ducked his head and closed his eyes. A shiver worked through him as he waited for Dixon's response.

"Helsinki," Dixon whispered, his warm breath wafting over the curve of his ear. "Look at me." Dixon slid a hand from his hip, up his chest, then wrapped it around his throat. "Turn your head, my mate, and meet my eyes."

Speared on Dixon's dick, even though his own shaft had begun to soften with nerves, Helsinki knew he couldn't get out of it. He allowed his mate to turn his head. Still, he struggled to lift his gaze to meet Dixon's eyes.

When Helsinki did, he gasped. The happiness shining from Dixon's blue orbs took his breath away. Dixon practically beamed with joy at him.

"D-Dixon?" Helsinki didn't understand Dixon's response. "I-I-I—"

"Helsinki, I love you, too," Dixon murmured before tipping his head and bussing an awkward kiss to his lips.

"Thank you for your love. I am so fucking blessed."

After swallowing to clear his surprise, Helsinki whispered, "You love me, too?"

Dixon nodded, smiling at him. "I love you, too, Hels." Then he began moving again, but he didn't stop talking. "You'd already been through so much, so many changes, and I didn't want to pressure you." After suckling on Helsinki's earlobe for a few ruts, pegging his gland with each slow glide, Dixon admitted, "I thought not saying anything would allow you to come to your own conclusions without pressure. Now I wonder if I did the right thing." Dixon nipped at his neck. "I'm sorry you were ever concerned about my feelings for you. I love you more than my own life, my mate."

Groaning, Helsinki blinked swiftly, forcing the moisture from his eyes. "I love you, too, Dix," he mumbled. "Read somewhere you weren't supposed to say it durin' sex, though."

Chuckling roughly, Dixon replied huskily, "You can say it any damn time you want, my mate." After licking up his neck, he added, "I love hearing it."

Helsinki grinned, his heart thudding wildly in his chest. "Then I'll say it a lot."

"Me, too." Then Dixon sped up his ruts. He adjusted his moves ever-so-slightly so he pegged Helsinki's gland head-on, over and over. "Now come, my mate," Dixon urged. "Fill your hand with your seed so we can enjoy it together."

Moaning with anticipation, Helsinki began jacking his cock. He felt his balls draw up, so he sped up his strokes. His chute muscles fluttered, milking the length giving him a sensual internal massage.

"Yessss, mate," Dixon hissed into his ear. "That's it. Come, Hels. Come. Clamp onto my cock, and milk my seed from me."

Helsinki gritted his teeth to hold in his howl of ecstasy created by the bliss of his balls pulling tight. Mind-numbing waves of endorphins caused his brain to short-circuit, and only Dixon's hand suddenly clamping over his mouth kept his cries from echoing through the room. Helsinki's warm spend began filling his hand, and he cupped his palm further, catching as much as possible.

Feeling Dixon's erection throb in his channel coupled with the heat of his wolf's seed flooding his body, Helsinki pulsed out one more burst of cum. He sagged against the door, resting his forehead on the back of his hand. His body shuddered with aftershocks as Dixon nibbled the back of his neck.

"Gods, you're perfect for me," Dixon mumbled against his flesh. "Love how you take care of me." Then he licked a stripe up Helsinki's sweat-soaked neck and hummed. "Time to take care of you."

Gently, Dixon eased his prick from Helsinki's body. Then he gripped Helsinki's waist and urged him to turn around, pressing his back into the door. The coolness caused a shiver to streak down his spine, but it felt fantastic since his body felt overheated from his work mucking stalls coupled with the awesome sex.

"Mmm-mmm," Dixon hummed, cradling Helsinki's hand with his own. "Look at this tasty treat."

Helsinki felt his heart speed up as Dixon guided his cum-filled hand to his wolf's mouth. Dixon held his gaze as he sipped at his spilled seed. After licking his lips, his mouth curving in a lascivious smile, Dixon pushed Helsinki's cupped hand to his own lips.

Dipping his head, Helsinki lapped at his spend. He hummed happily, enjoying his lightly salty flavor. There were traces of something peppery in there, too, but he'd never been able to figure out how to describe it.

Dixon didn't seem to mind and had never commented on

it.

After Helsinki took another drink of himself, Dixon pulled his hand back to his own mouth. He finished Helsinki's seed, even licking his palm and between his fingers. Feeling Dixon's tongue sliding over his flesh, cleaning him and getting every drop, almost caused his prick to thicken once more.

Only hearing the sound of masculine voices kept Helsinki's dick semi-soft.

"Any idea where Dixon ended up?" Leonard — Leo to his friends — asked. "Galahad has been dozing in the cross-ties for about fifteen minutes now."

Dixon chuckled softly into Helsinki's ear. "Guess we've been in here long enough," he murmured, revealing he'd heard the voices, too. "Let's go ride, my love." As Dixon straightened and turned on the faucet while grabbing some paper towels, he drew his brows together. "Hope you're not too sore to ride?"

Helsinki cleared his throat as he thought about that. Being sore hadn't even occurred to him. "I'll be okay," he assured. *Whatever it takes.*

"You sure?" Dixon asked as he wiped his half-hard prick with the damp towels, cleaning himself. "We can reschedule."

"No way I wanna miss riding with you," Helsinki stated with fervor. "You've never hurt me before, and that hasn't changed now."

Helsinki didn't consider the stretch of being taken by his lover to be him causing him pain.

Dixon eyed him for a few seconds as he tossed the soiled paper towels into the garbage. After righting his riding breeches, he dampened several more. "Okay," he said with a nod. "Let me clean you up, and we'll get out there. There's an awesome trail I want to take you on today. The views are fantastic."

More than on board with that, Helsinki submitted to his mate's ministrations, all the while willing his prick not to reharden as he enjoyed their intimacy.

CHAPTER ELEVEN

"How's he settling in?" Alpha Declan asked as he handed Dixon a cup of tea. "Been two weeks, right?"

Dixon nodded as he brought the steaming liquid to his lips. After enjoying a small sip of the brew, discovering it was Earl Grey, he hummed happily. Relaxing into the sofa, Dixon watched as his alpha settled on a comfortable chair to his right.

"Yeah, two weeks yesterday," Dixon told his alpha, a smile toying at the corners of his lips as he thought of his mate. "He's been a surprise. That's for sure."

Declan chuckled, resting his mug of coffee on the arm of his chair. "I'll say. When Councilman Goldstein contacted me and told me that ye'd found yer mate, I was happy for ye." Then Declan's black brows furrowed. "Of course, then he told me a little about Helsinki, and I admit, it had me a wee bit worried. Found protectin' one of the rogue ex-councilmen."

Dixon nodded once, accepting and understanding his alpha's concerns. "I hear ya." Placing his mug on his thigh, he rubbed the back of his neck. "Of course, then you have one conversation with him and realize—"

Snapping his mouth shut, Dixon shook his head. He struggled with how to finish his thought. His overall assessment of his mate had changed after living with him for a couple of weeks.

"First impression is he's a little dim, isn't it?" Alpha Declan prodded. "But that's not really the case."

"Funny how first impressions can be so very wrong, huh?"

94

Dixon murmured, thinking about the truth of his mate. "He's just so damn family-oriented. Learned it from his mom. Family first, family second, and family to the end." Rolling his eyes, Dixon muttered, "It makes him a little naive, and Rian took advantage of that in the worst way."

"Fortunately, family can mean more than just blood," Declan pointed out. "How's he doing with Gordon?"

Dixon smirked, having should have known that his alpha would know that he'd convinced Helsinki to go into therapy. "Doing well," he claimed. "Although I can't tell you specifics."

Declan lifted a hand and shook his head. "Aye, that I know. Just wanted to be certain he's doing okay." While his expression turned contemplative, he lifted his mug to his lips and drank his coffee.

Cocking his head, Dixon wondered what his alpha was thinking. He waited patiently, sipping his tea. Fortunately, he didn't have too long to wait. His alpha wasn't one to draw things out. Declan was far more direct, choosing not to play pointless mind games with his people.

In Dixon's opinion, it made him a fantastic alpha to follow — fair and even-tempered.

Dixon had shared a couple of conversations with Shane Alvaro when he'd been in Savannah. The former Stone Ridge beta turned councilman had offered him an interesting view of the pack. As the right hand of the fairly laid-back alpha — an alpha who had to be pushed pretty hard to lose his temper — Shane had been the one to act as an overbearing asshole at times as he kept a finger on the pulse of the pack.

It had been a fantastic educational moment, and Dixon had been keeping an eye on things to see if he needed to follow in the ex-beta's footsteps.

Good thing I don't mind being a hard-ass at times.

"I received a call from Regales this morning."

Ah, here's why Alpha Declan called me over first thing this morning.

"Something to do with Helsinki's brother?" Dixon guessed, tension tightening his spine. "Or one of the bastard's friends?"

Declan sighed deeply. "Afraid so."

Dixon gritted his teeth, his wolf growling in his mind at the mention of the man who'd caused his mate so much pain. Reaching into his shirt pocket, he pulled out a toothpick and popped it into his mouth. Dixon rolled it between his teeth, rubbing the tip of his tongue over the point.

His upset wolf settled, perceiving the light chewing of the toothpick as gnawing on a bone in animal form. His beast found it relaxing. Being such a dominant shifter, he'd discovered the technique almost a century ago to keep his animal calm in high-tension situations.

There was damn near always a small twig, blade of grass, or even a piece of ice that would suffice as a distraction when his wolf became annoyed at something . . . or someone . . . and he couldn't pacify him by shifting and chewing on a bone.

"Try not to take my head off when I tell ye this next bit, hmm?" Declan commented, obviously having picked up on his habit.

Dixon smirked as he shrugged. "I can promise to take my annoyance out in a safe manner." Scoffing, he shook his head. "And of course I wouldn't try to take your head off. No way I'd want to run this pack without you."

Barking a laugh, Declan rolled his eyes. He met his gaze, his gray eyes sparkling with mirth. Unfortunately, that changed swiftly enough.

"Well, it seems Rian decided to try to petition the council to force Helsinki to pay for lost revenue, since when he was paying penance for working for the rogue, yer mate lost his job." Declan spoke quickly, obviously trying to get it all out. "He claimed that, without his brother's revenue, he's struggling financially, and he could lose his home."

Growling low in his throat, Dixon clamped his teeth together. He felt the toothpick snap and pulled the loose end from between his lips. With a flick of his fingers, he tossed it into a nearby garbage can while he chewed up the small bit that had been left in his mouth. Dixon swigged his tea, washing it down, trying to stop himself from grabbing his phone and calling Regales himself to demand to know what the fuck had happened.

"Breathe, Dixon," Alpha Declan ordered, a low growl rumbling through his words. "I'm not done."

Dixon finished his tea, then set his mug on the end table. Blowing out a breath, he focused on Declan. He jerked a nod.

"Sorry. Rian is just—" Dixon shook his head as he rubbed one hand over his face. "What an overbearing asshole piece of work."

"I believe ye," Declan assured, resting his coffee mug on his knee. "And evidently, so do a lot of others on the council. Enforcer Delanrue spoke up and shared how Rian had been stealing quite a bit of Helsinki's paycheck for years." Narrowing his eyes, Declan growled softly as he continued speaking, "Then Investigator Jensen shared a report about how Rian was participating in an illegal fighting ring, beating up unwitting humans for cash."

"Please tell me the fucker is in council custody," Dixon snarled, hope flooding him. As much as he didn't want to have to share that sort of information with his mate, he would gladly do it if it meant Rian would be out of their hair for . . . well, a very long time.

Declan's expression turned pained as he shook his head. "Afraid not."

Jumping from his seat, Dixon roared, "Why the hell not?"

Lifting his hand in placation, Declan also rose to his feet. His alpha set his mug aside so he could place both of his hands on Dixon's shoulders. At six-three, Declan stared him in the eye, his gray eyes dark, expressing his own anger at the situation.

"Ye know that his buddy Mason is a tracker for the council."

Dixon nodded. "Right. He's under review."

"Aye, that he is," Declan confirmed. "Although after his actions of last night, being under review has turned into being a wanted shifter."

Glaring to the left—one did not glare at his alpha—Dixon asked between clenched teeth, "What happened?"

Declan tightened his hold on Dixon's shoulders as he told him, "Rian was ordered to take a mandatory shifter education course, and he was also ordered to turn over all his financial data for the last decade."

Dixon snorted. "Bet that didn't go over well."

"It did not, and Rian pretty much screamed that, too." Declan frowned. "Somethin' about how if his dumb-ass brother hadn't stolen his inheritance, none of this would have happened?"

Shaking his head, Dixon grumbled, "When their mother passed, everything went to Rian except one piece of jewelry. A brooch." He couldn't help but smile as he thought of the happy expression on Helsinki's face every time he looked at the pretty—and expensive—item. "I really doubt Helsinki realizes the true value of the massive pin. It's made of this huge ruby with green emeralds around it in this gorgeous weave of gold filigree." Thinking of Helsinki and his fondness when talking of his mother and the pin, Dixon found his ire easing. "Anyway, he looks at the pin and sees his mother. He doesn't give a shit what its monetary value is."

"And when *Rian* thinks of the brooch, money is *all* he sees," Declan guessed.

Dixon nodded. "That'd be my guess. While Helsinki was living at the council headquarters, Rian tossed his room in the house they shared searching for it." Thinking of Helsinki's hiding place, Dixon chuckled. "One thing I can say for Hels, my mate knows how to hide things." Cocking his head, he admitted, "Come to think of it, I have absolutely no idea where he's tucked the thing at home. I offered a safety deposit box, but he declined." Dixon shrugged, meeting his alpha's gaze. "Guess he likes to take it out and look at it sometimes."

Declan nodded, his smile turning a little wistful. "I'm glad he has some happy memories of his mother." Just that quick, his alpha cleared his throat and released him. "Anyway, when Rian was being led to his *rooms* at headquarters" — Declan lifted his fingers and made air quotes — "Mason shot Germaine, and the pair fled."

Recalling the tall, wiry python shifter, Dixon blurted, "Is Germaine okay?" He'd only met the guy briefly, but he'd seemed a decent sort.

Arching one black brow, Declan dipped his chin in a nod. "It was touch and go for a few hours, but aye, he'll make a full recovery."

"Good," Dixon muttered, frowning. "So, Rian and Mason are on the run." Rubbing his chin, he mused, "Did anyone check Tanner's place?"

Declan rested his hands on his hips as he shrugged. "They told me they checked all the homes of his known friends," he explained. "But no one seems to have any knowledge of where he is."

Dixon groaned as the realization hit him. "That means he's headed this way," he mumbled, rubbing his hands over his face. His wolf howled and snarled in his mind. The urge to shift and track down his mate hit Dixon hard, and he struggled to beat it back. Breathing raggedly, he grumbled, "He blames Helsinki because he got away, so he's going to come after him."

"Breathe, Dixon," Declan urged, drawing him into his embrace. "Settle yer wolf. I can drive ye home far faster than ye can run."

As Declan spoke, he gripped Dixon's nape with one hand. He pulled him closer, even going so far as tucking Dixon's face into his neck. With his other hand, Declan rubbed up and down Dixon's back.

To Dixon's surprise, as he breathed in Declan's scent and sank into his alpha's soothing embrace, his wolf settled. He couldn't remember ever seeing or experiencing an alpha relaxing a pack-member before. While Dixon had always respected his new alpha, the fact that Declan would take the time to help him settle brought his respect to a whole new level.

Dixon sighed, giving in to his odd urge and resting his forehead on Declan's shoulder. "Gods, I don't recall ever seeing an alpha settle someone this way," he mumbled. He figured he would be embarrassed about his outburst later.

Right then, Dixon just didn't care.

Declan massaged Dixon's nape lightly while murmuring softly, "I saw my grandfather soothe upset pack-members just like this for decades, Dixon. Sadly, I think it's becoming a lost art form because too many alphas have decided they're supposed to be big and bad and rule by fear and intimidation." Gripping Dixon's neck, Declan urged him to lift his head, and their gazes clashed. His alpha smirked. "It's really the opposite, ye know? An alpha serves his pack-members just as much as his pack serves him."

Dixon grimaced a bit wanly. "I think you're right."

Giving him a warm smile, Declan stated, "Maybe we'll find a way to bring this technique back into the mainstream." Then he eased his hold on Dixon, and they both straightened. "Come on, then. I don't see ye as fit to drive, so let me take ye home."

Even as Dixon followed his alpha out of his office, he had to ask, "Are you certain you have time for that?"

He knew exactly how busy his alpha normally was.

Declan scoffed softly. "Actually, I'd love the distraction," he admitted. "Lark is at Edwin's, checking out some new concoction," he told him. "And with Sara officially mated and living with her man closer to Colin City" — Declan paused and sighed, shaking his head — "the house is quiet on my day off."

Dixon nodded, following Declan from the large lodge-style home. He knew Lark — the alpha's mate — enjoyed working with Edwin, who was a human scientist who'd been raised by a cougar shifter. With Lark being a doctor, the pair met up and discussed not only how to use shifter blood and genetics to perhaps someday aid human healing, but they also developed herbal medicines that could withstand a shifter's metabolism.

As Dixon settled in the passenger seat of Declan's truck — he figured he could have Helsinki bring him by later that evening to grab his own vehicle — he clicked on his seatbelt.

Before Declan had even managed to get the truck out of his driveway, his phone chimed. When he brought up the screen on his truck's display showing who was calling, he arched one brow. As he turned his truck onto the road, Declan connected the call.

"Morning, Lyle," Declan greeted. "Ye have me and Dixon."

"Good," Lyle replied without preamble. "Because I'm with Grady at Caribou's, eating lunch, and we see Helsinki on the other side of the restaurant." His concern came through loud and clear in his tone. "He's sitting with someone who looks sort of similar to him, and we don't like the body language."

"Fuck," Dixon growled. "Rian's here already."

"Who's Rian?" Lyle asked immediately. "What can we do to help?"

That was what Dixon loved about this pack. Everyone was

willing to lend a hand when needed.

"Rian is Helsinki's no good, bigoted, asshole of a brother," Declan told him. "Oh, and he's a wanted man."

Lyle's hissing growl came through the phone. "You don't say?"

"Indeed," Declan confirmed. "Ye wouldn't mind staying with him until we arrive, would ye? We're already on the road."

"No place we'd rather be," Lyle claimed. "I haven't officially met Helsinki, yet. I think I'll go introduce myself."

"He could have a buddy or two with him," Dixon warned. "We're on our way."

Grady's deep voice came through the line. "I'll scout the area and make certain no one else is about."

"Thanks," Dixon answered earnestly.

"Pack is family," Grady claimed, then the line disconnected.

"Fuck," Dixon mumbled.

Declan reached over and gripped his wrist, squeezing lightly for a few seconds. "Yer mate will be fine. Our pack will keep him safe."

Dixon nodded, doing his best to believe it. There was one thing he knew for certain. "I'm going to paddle Helsinki's ass for not calling me before meeting his brother at Caribou's."

What the hell was my mate thinking?

Except, Dixon thought he knew.

Family first.

CHAPTER TWELVE

Helsinki knew he'd made a horrible mistake, but now he didn't know how to fix it. When his brother had called him on the phone — *how had he gotten my new number, anyway* — he'd been too shocked to ask too many questions. Then, hearing Rian's friendly tone and request to apologize in person, Helsinki had agreed to meet with him.

At least I didn't give him my address like he'd asked.

At first, Rian had wanted to meet Helsinki at his house. He'd asked to come over. Helsinki hadn't been comfortable with that, especially since Dixon was in a meeting with Alpha Declan.

So, Helsinki had decided to meet Rian at a bar and grill restaurant in town. He'd thought it would be okay. After all, it was a public place.

Except, after the first five minutes, where they'd ordered their drinks and meals, Rian had started explaining why all the bad things happening to him in life were all Helsinki's fault.

After going to counseling several times a week with Gordon, Helsinki had understood what Rian was trying to do. His brother was trying to guilt-trip him into agreeing to help him. Except, Helsinki knew that was wrong.

One of the first things Rian had told him was how he'd had to flee home because people on the council were ordering him to take some dumb-ass, brain-washing class. That meant his brother was on the run. Helsinki knew he wasn't the brightest crayon in the box — although he no longer thought of himself as dumb—and he realized that meant Rian was a fugitive to the council.

"Why don't you want to take the class?" Helsinki asked when there was a lull in Rian's hissed ranting.

If looks could kill, Helsinki would be dead.

Rian glared angrily at him. Leaning across the table as far as he could, he snarled, "Weren't you listening, you dumb fuck? It's a brain-washing course." Then his lip curled. "Is that why you decided to fuck a guy after everything I taught you? Did they put you through it?" Shaking his head, Rian grumbled, "You come with us. We'll straighten you out again."

Helsinki felt his blood run cold.

Us. We.

My brother isn't alone.

Even as Helsinki wondered who Rian was referring to—he could make a couple of guesses—the waitress arrived with the food. At least that gave him a momentary reprieve. Rian sat back in his booth seat so the waitress could place the food before them.

Helsinki asked for a bottle of ketchup, since he'd ordered a burger and fries. Plus, that meant the woman would be returning shortly. He had every intention of having his strawberry lemonade finished by then, so she would swing around once more.

As much as Helsinki hated monopolizing the waitress in that way, he needed as much interference as he could get.

Maybe the waitress will distract Rian a little, and I can send a text to Dixon.

Helsinki hadn't wanted to bother his mate while in a meeting with Alpha Declan. That would have been rude. Plus, he'd thought everything would be okay.

Boy, was I wrong.

After Julia had walked away, Rian ordered, "Hurry up and eat fast. We should get out of here."

Even as Helsinki's bear rumbled with worry in the back of

his mind, worry that he shared with his animal, he silently vowed, "No fucking way."

Instead of hurrying—considering Rian had picked up his burger and was shoving it into his face as if he hadn't eaten in days—Helsinki picked up his roll of fabric-covered silverware. He unrolled it and placed the napkin on his lap. Then Helsinki grabbed his knife and fork.

Carefully, Helsinki cut his bacon cheeseburger in half. He'd just returned his silverware to the table when a shadow fell over his table. Looking up, Helsinki cocked his head. He didn't recognize the dark-haired man standing there.

From the scowl on Rian's face, Helsinki didn't think his brother did, either.

"Hey, it's Helsinki Akna, right?" the guy greeted with a grin, showing off even white teeth. Once Helsinki nodded, the stranger held out his hand. "I'm Lyle Sullivan. Dixon is a friend."

Helsinki slowly took the guy's hand.

To Helsinki's surprise, the man held on as he stated, "Sorry, I couldn't make it to Dixon's welcome home party." He rolled his eyes. "Work."

In truth, Dixon's *welcome home* party had actually been a *congratulations on your mating* barbeque. Did that mean this guy wasn't a shifter? He remembered Dixon mentioning a Lyle, but he couldn't remember in what context. There were too many people in the wolf pack . . . not to mention those humans in town that his mate occasionally worked with as a park ranger—law enforcement, search and rescue personnel, and those in the medical field.

"Hey, man, we're—" Rian began to cut in.

The guy immediately snapped his attention to Rian and offered him a toothy grin. "Lyle. Lyle Sullivan."

Rian narrowed his eyes and sniffed deeply, as if inhaling slowly. To Helsinki, it was obvious Rian was trying to scent the man. Curling his lip, Rian snapped, "We're in the middle of lunch, Lyle, so move along."

The stranger, Lyle, either didn't notice or didn't care that Rian clearly didn't want him there. He did finally release Helsinki as he turned his attention back to him.

"Hey, I don't mean to interrupt," Lyle commented, making Helsinki think he was about to excuse himself.

Too bad.

Then, to Helsinki's amazement, Lyle settled on the bench seat next to him. On instinct, Helsinki moved over, making more room for the man. Finally, with the guy so close, he managed to get a big whiff of the guy's scent.

What the fuck?

Helsinki had never scented anything like Lyle. He smelled of shifter . . . sort of. There was also something . . . else, too. The aroma had almost a . . . metallic component to it . . . or maybe chemical.

Lyle winked at Helsinki, breaking him out of his confused stupor. "Anyway, I won't stop you from eating your lunch," he told him, motioning toward Helsinki's burger. "I just thought I'd stop by for a moment to get to know you, is all." Lyle's grin widened. "Oh, and my husband, Todd, he loves to put on dinner parties. You and Dixon need to come to the next one." Tapping the table, he offered, "Give me your number, and I'll text you the info to the next one."

For some reason, Helsinki thought that scented of a lie. Still, the man was another buffer between him and his brother, so he would play along. Pulling out his phone, he handed it over.

"Thanks." Lyle began tapping away at his phone. He hummed as he did so, completely unconcerned with the death-glares he was receiving from Rian across the table. "Here ya go." Lyle handed the phone back.

On instinct, Helsinki glanced at it. For a second, he froze. Then he quickly read the message on the screen.

Dixon is pissed you met with your brother without calling him first. Rian is a wanted man. Your mate's on his way. Don't worry, Hels. You're surrounded by pack. We got your back.

Helsinki did his best not to react to the news, but he couldn't help a little bit of a relieved sigh. Glancing at Lyle, he tried to think up something to say as he put his phone away.

It wasn't until Helsinki took a swig of his strawberry lemonade a good thirty seconds later that he managed to come up with anything. "Um, so, how do you know Dixon?" Realizing how open-ended that could be, he quickly added, "Are you a park ranger, too?"

"No, I'm—"

Rian growled as he leaned forward. "Hey," he interrupted. His dark eyes were narrowed into slits as he sneered at Lyle. "Look, asshole, you're interrupting lunch with my brother, so why don't you get lost?"

Lyle slowly turned his attention toward Rian. He furrowed his brows and dipped his chin a little. His scent spiked a little, betraying his annoyance.

For just an instant, Rian's dominant countenance slipped. He straightened, moving away from Lyle. A second later, he seemed to regain his bravado. With one hand, Rian picked up his burger, and with his other, he waved negligently toward the front door of the restaurant.

To Helsinki's shock, Lyle tipped his head back and laughed. His grin stretched from ear to ear. The man even went so far as to shake his head, as if he thought Rian's actions were the funniest shit . . . ever.

Helsinki figured he would have continued staring in shock. Except, Julia returned with his ketchup. She smiled as she placed the bottle on the table, her attention shifting to Lyle.

As Julia straightened, she greeted him. "Hey, Detective. Switched tables on us, huh?" She grinned broadly. "Can I get ya anything?"

"An unsweetened iced tea would be fantastic, Jules," Lyle replied. Then he winked and added, "Maybe a piece of that carrot cake, too."

Humming, Julia nodded. "You got it, sugar." Then she headed away.

Once Julia was far enough away, Lyle turned back to Rian. His grin turned feral. "Well, Rian, now that the cat is out of the bag, let's not make a scene in front of the humans." Leaning on the table, he pointed toward the door. "How about you stand up and head right that way. I'll be a couple of steps behind you."

Rian curled his lip, and his nostrils flared. "How about I pull out my gun, wave it around, and start shooting." Showing off a canine, he declared, "I don't mind takin' some fag detective out along with a few worthless humans."

"He's not alone," Helsinki blurted out, earning him a growl from Rian. After so much time with people who actually cared about him, Helsinki ignored Rian's not-so-silent threat. "At least one, but maybe more."

Lyle glanced his way for just a second before he smirked at Rian. "I know. Grady and a couple of others probably have them well in hand by now." Narrowing his eyes, Lyle pinned a cold stare on Rian. "Stand up, keep your hands at your sides, and walk out the front door."

"Fuck you!" Rian screamed, lunging out of the booth and to his feet.

Helsinki cringed back, huddling against the wall as he spotted the gun his brother whipped from . . . somewhere.

Lyle jumped up, shoving the table forward. The move caused the corner to slam into Rian's hip, making him stagger. The other shifter was on him instantly.

The gun went off, and Lyle jolted.

While Helsinki wasn't too proud of it, he whimpered.

Somehow, Lyle still managed to wrestle the gun from

Rian's grip. He slammed his brother's torso onto the skewed table, securing him in place. As Lyle slapped a pair of cuffs on Rian, his brother glared at him.

"This is all your fault," Rian snarled. "You should have obeyed."

Helsinki shook his head slowly. "None of this is my fault," he murmured. While he wasn't able to raise his voice, he managed to keep his tone level and firm. "*You* made your own decisions. I'm not responsible for *any* of them."

"Fuck you, you worthless piece of dumb-ass fag shit!" Rian roared as Lyle heaved him to his feet. "You ruined everything. You —"

"And that's enough of that," Lyle grumbled as he stuffed a handkerchief into Rian's mouth. He turned a kind smile Helsinki's way as he told him, "Come on out with me. I'm sure Dixon will be here by now and will want to know you're safe."

Helsinki nodded and rose to his feet. Pausing, he glanced at the table with the food strewn all over it and the drinks spilled across the wood. He wondered if he had enough cash to leave to cover everything.

"Hels." Lyle calling his name pulled him out of his musing. "I'll let Julia know to put it on my tab. Don't you worry about a thing."

Nodding, Helsinki started toward Lyle. He didn't have a clue what kind of shifter the detective was, but his bear recognized him as damn dominant. The man's orders were easy to follow.

How does Declan deal with that in his territory?

Even as Helsinki wondered that, he followed Lyle out of the restaurant. A second later, his silent question was answered.

Mutual respect, he realized.

Declan and Dixon were both striding across the parking lot — Dixon doing more of a jog — and Lyle immediately dipped his head in acknowledgment of them both.

"Hey, guys," Lyle greeted, lifting his head. "Sorry. You missed the action."

Declan grinned as he swept his gaze over everyone. "All is well, then, my friend?" he asked, refocusing on Lyle.

Lyle nodded. "All is well." Then he scowled. "Until you un-muzzle this asshole."

While Declan snorted and assured, "We'll deal," Dixon grabbed Helsinki, pulling his attention away from the pair.

"Are you injured?" Dixon asked, rubbing his hands all over Helsinki's torso and arms, obviously searching for injury. "I heard a gunshot."

"I'm good," Helsinki assured, sinking into Dixon's embrace. "I'm so sorry. Rian called, and I thought—" He cut himself off and shook his head. "Whatever I thought was foolishness." Meeting Dixon's worried gaze, Helsinki admitted, "Misplaced hope."

"He's your brother," Dixon whispered, revealing with those simple words that he understood.

Helsinki nodded. "Yeah."

Dixon pressed a kiss to Helsinki's lips, slow and lingering, and Helsinki loved every second of it.

When Dixon lifted his head, he traced along Helsinki's jaw lovingly. "So, no one got shot?"

"Um." Now that Helsinki thought about it, he wasn't so sure. "Lyle was fighting with Rian for the gun."

Glancing Lyle's way, where the man had just put a trussed Rian in the back of an SUV with an equally tied up Mason and Tanner, who were being watched over by Carson, Manon, and another enforcer named Kade, Dixon called, "You good, Lyle? Get shot?"

Lyle rolled his eyes as he slammed the door closed. "Of course, I got shot." He lifted his shirt at his belly to reveal a swarthy, dark-brown swath of . . . vest, skin, shirt . . . Helsinki had no idea. Lyle rapped on the tough material. "But I'm armored." As he put down his shirt, he grimaced. "Don't tell Todd."

Dixon laughed. "Hell, Lyle. You know Todd'll find out, but I'll bring you the finest rum as a thank you to placate him."

A look of relief filled Lyle's expression even as he grinned. "Now you're talkin'!"

Grinning, Dixon focused on Helsinki and began leading him toward another vehicle. "Lyle is good."

Helsinki nodded. Glancing around, he couldn't help but lean close and whisper, "What is he?"

Shaking his head, Dixon murmured back, "I'll tell you all about Lyle . . . after I take you home and paddle your ass." Then his gaze turned heated. "After I wash you in the shower and check you over for injury."

While Helsinki wasn't so certain what to think about the paddling idea, he still nodded. After all, his heart was beating wildly upon hearing the showering and inspection aspect.

After Dixon helped him into the passenger seat of a vehicle that looked suspiciously like Alpha Declan's, his mate rubbed his thigh. "Just know this for now, huh?"

Helsinki cocked his head, waiting.

"Lyle is pack. He's family." Dixon leveled a serious gaze on Helsinki. "Our pack is the family we're making it to be."

Liking the sound of that, Helsinki nodded and grinned. "Yeah. That sounds about perfect."

"Good."

Then Dixon kissed him hard before taking a step backward and closing him into the cab.

Helsinki watched Dixon trot around the front of the truck, then climb behind the wheel. As they headed home, leaving the flurry of activity behind, he knew he would see them all again soon enough. After all, they were his new family.

Reaching over, Helsinki took Dixon's hand in his own,

knowing the man beside him was the best part of that.

You may also enjoy the following from eXtasy Books Inc:

A Gargoyle of His Own
Charlie Richards

Excerpt

"Speaking of which," Krispin commented before knocking back the rest of his whiskey. "It's getting late. I'm going to head up. I'll have my phone on me if anything arises that needs my attention."

Basques nodded. He was on management duty that evening. They rotated it between the three of them, so no one ended up burned out.

"Have a good one, Kris," Ridger A Wolf in Hiding offered before sweeping his gaze over the lounge. "I don't see what I'm after in here, so I think I'll head to the dance club." He waggled his brows and licked his lips.

Chuckling, Basques patted Ridger on his shoulder. "Happy hunting, my friend."

Krispin paused, watching Ridger head out of the room. He knew what his buddy planned to do. His vampire second was looking for a little action so he could feed.

Turning back to Basques, Krispin asked, "I bet you don't miss that, do you?"

Basques shook his head, a warm smile creasing the features as a faraway light entered his eyes. "Definitely not."

A pang of jealousy churned in Krispin's gut, and he quickly squashed it. He didn't want Dloben, but he did want what his head enforcer had found. At over two hundred years old, he was getting a little tired of waiting.

And, yet, continue to wait, I shall.

Krispin headed out of the lounge and crossed to the elevator. Inserting a key card into the slot, he hit the button for floor thirteen. He and his inner circle lived on the first floor above the humans—first line of defense and secrecy.

The vampire covens' floors could only be accessed with a key card.

Once Krispin reached his suite, he headed straight for the bedroom, unbuttoning his suite jacket on the way. He tossed his wallet, keys, card, and phone on the nightstand. After that, he quickly stripped, placing his dirty clothes into the hamper.

Krispin took a short, hot shower, happy to wash off the stress of the day. After drying, he grabbed a pair of pale green lounging pants. He picked up his phone and keycard, slid his feet into a pair of house shoes, then left his suite.

The private elevator Krispin headed to could only be accessed by a select few, since it was the only one that reached the roof. Stepping inside, anticipation filled him. He inserted his keycard before tapping the button for the roof.

As soon as the door swished open, revealing the warm evening, Krispin inhaled deeply. The fragrance of flowers, earth, and bushes filled his senses. The trickle of the fountain reached his ears. Soft lights revealed the maze of the garden paths as well as the colorful plants.

Krispin smiled.

Stepping off the elevator, Krispin headed down a path to his right. His friend's assessment—rooftop oasis—really was accurate. He loved it up there.

Pausing at a storage closet set up against the wall of the greenhouse, Krispin pulled out his yoga mat. His penchant for yoga and meditation wasn't common knowledge in his coven. He liked to keep that little personal nugget to himself and a few trusted people—namely, Ridger, Basques, and now Dloben.

It wasn't that he was embarrassed by his nightly ritual. Instead, he just didn't care for the teasing he knew it would invite. What he got up to in private was his own business.

Placing the yoga mat on a grassy stretch near the fountain, Krispin stepped onto it and began his nightly routine. As he moved through different poses, focusing on his breathing and headspace, he felt the troubles of the day slip away. His mind cleared, and the muscles of his body warmed.

Perfect.

Krispin was just wrapping up his routine when an odd whooshing sound reached his sensitive ears. Cocking his head, he straightened and rested his hands on his hips. He narrowed his eyes and waited to see if it came again.

It did, accompanied by the unmistakable sound of flesh hitting flesh and a roar.

"What the hell?" Krispin peered around, searching for the source. "Who's fighting at my coven?"

To Krispin's shock, movement to his right drew his attention just in time to watch a large form slam into a trellis, wiping it out. The body continued to tumble, carving a trail of dirt and destruction. A blueberry bush went next, followed by a bed of daylilies. Finally, the brown-skinned form came to a stop beside a pecan tree.

Krispin started toward it warily. He spotted black wings, and realized he was staring at a gargoyle.

What the hell?

He was within twenty feet of the male when another gargoyle landed next to the fallen one. Instead of helping, the gray-hided gargoyle swung a black-clawed hand and flayed the skin of the brown gargoyle's back. Blood sprayed from the wound . . . hitting Krispin in the face and torso.

Licking his lips at it on reflex, Krispin discovered two

things at once.

My beloved just fell from the sky right in front of me, and some motherfucker is trying to kill him.

Hell no!

Screaming a battle cry, Krispin lunged. With his vampire speed, he easily reached the attacker between one heartbeat and the next. He sliced his claws through one black wing as he sank the claws of the other into the gargoyle's back, right about where the kidney should be.

The gargoyle belled and lunged forward, jumping away from Krispin. He pivoted and spread his thick arms and wide wings.

"Stay out of this, vampire," the male ordered.

"You landed on the roof of my coven house," Krispin stated. "No unsanctioned attacks will take place here. State your name and business."

No way was he going to tell the bastard of his discovery. He didn't know what was going on between the two males, but he wasn't going to allow him to hurt his beloved.

Sneering, the gargoyle stated, "As if you could stop me."

The male lunged forward, but Krispin was ready. He pivoted and swung, slicing his three-inch talons into the gargoyle's side. The male was clumsy, thinking his massive, six-foot-six frame gave him an advantage.

Krispin hadn't kept hold of his coven for one-hundred-fifty years with words alone. He'd been in his fair share of fights. He easily evaded the gargoyle's attempts to hit him, countering with blows to the creature's torso, thighs, and wings each time.

After Krispin's third slash to the gargoyle's wings, the other paranormal bellowed with rage as he lifted off the ground. At first, Krispin thought he would dive-bomb him or something. Instead, he flew away, yelling that it wasn't over.

Krispin watched the gargoyle until he was out of sight in the dark sky.

"Moron doesn't even know if he's being watched by a human," Krispin grumbled, shaking his head. "What the fuck?"

Then a low moan caught his attention, returning his focus to his downed beloved.

Rushing to the male's side, Krispin took in the flayed hide of his back and one wing. He grimaced as he knelt beside him. As much as he wished he could begin licking the wounds to seal them, he didn't know the male or what had brought him here.

But I will soon.

The fact that he hadn't woken, yet was cause for concern, too.

"Right, get my head out of my ass."

Krispin jumped to his feet and rushed back to his yoga mat. He grabbed his phone and dialed Basques's number. His enforcer picked up on the second ring just as Krispin dropped back to his knees beside the gargoyle.

"Hey, buddy," Basques greeted. "All's quiet here. No need to—"

"Shut up a sec," Krispin cut him off. "I need you to locate Ward and bring him and Dloben up to the roof. Ridger, too, if he's not with a donor."

"I'm on the move," Basques replied instantly, and the noise of the lounge disappeared from the background. "I'll bring everyone up as quickly as I can. What's going on?"

Unable to touch, Krispin threaded his fingers through the gargoyle's shaggy, dark-brown hair, pushing it away from his face. "My mate just fell from the sky. Literally."

"What the fuck?"

Krispin felt about the same. "He's a gargoyle. He was attacked, and he's injured. Unconscious. I was wondering if Dloben would recognize him."

"Damn, Kris," Basques muttered through the line. "Congrats, and don't worry. I'm sure he'll be fine." Then a laugh erupted from him.

"What?" Krispin didn't know what his buddy could find

funny about the situation.

"Guess you're stuck carryin' your offspring, just like me."

Krispin felt his gut twist and his ass clench. Gargoyles could get their male mates pregnant.

"Oh fuck."

ABOUT THE AUTHOR

Charlie started writing fantasy when she was eight, and after stumbling onto her first erotic romance at age nineteen, she realized her true calling. She now focuses on writing gay erotic romance, normally of the paranormal variety, with heroes of all kinds. With the help and support of her husband, Charlie finally fulfilled one of her life-long goals . . . move to acreage with her horses. You can often find her curled up with her laptop and a cup of tea or glass of wine, creating her next adventure. Charlie enjoys exploring the mountains of her new Oregon home on horseback, 4-wheeler, or motorcycle.

She can be reached at ch.richards2010@yahoo.com

Or visit her at www.charlie-richards.com

www.ingramcontent.com/pod-product-compliance
Lightning Source LLC
Chambersburg PA
CBHW060639130626
46555CB00002B/875